Pirate in the Mist: Brody

Book 1

By

Elizabeth Rose

ISBN – 13: 978-1977767134
ISBN – 10: 1977767133

Books by Elizabeth Rose:

♛ (Legacy of the Blade Series)
♛ Prequel
♛ Lord of the Blade – Book 1
♛ Lady Renegade – Book 2
♛ Lord of Illusion – Book 3
♛ Lady of the Mist – Book 4

♗ (Daughters of the Dagger Series)
♗ Prequel
♗ Ruby – Book 1
♗ Sapphire – Book 2
♗ Amber – Book 3
♗ Amethyst – Book 4

♜ (MadMan MacKeefe Series)
♜ Onyx – Book 1
♜ Aidan – Book 2
♜ Ian – Book 3

✳ (Elemental Series)
✳ The Dragon and the DreamWalker: Book 1, Fire
✳ The Duke and the Dryad: Book 2, Earth
✳ The Sword and the Sylph: Book 3, Air
✳ The Sheik and the Siren: Book 4, Water

♞ (Greek Myth Fantasy)
♞ Kyros' Secret
♞ The Oracle of Delphi
♞ Thief of Olympus
♞ The Pandora Curse

Visit http://elizabethrosenovels.com

Author's Note:

This is the first book of my **Second in Command Series**. The series stems from secondary characters from some of my books. This is Brody's story. Brody is Rowen's first mate in **Restless Sea Lord**. Since it is a continuation of the **Legendary Bastards of the Crown Series**, it is best to read that series first to recognize some of the characters and so surprises from those books are not ruined by reading this first. It is also advised to read **Autumn – Book 3** of my **Seasons of Fortitude Series** first if possible, as there is a surprise in the epilogue that has to do with that book. However, this book also stands alone, so it is your choice.

The books in the Legendary Bastards of the Crown series are:

> **Destiny's Kiss – Series Prequel**
> **Restless Sea Lord – Book 1**
> **Ruthless Knight – Book 2**
> **Reckless Highlander – Book 3**

This is followed by the Seasons of Fortitude Series:

> **Highland Spring – Book 1**
> **Summer's Reign – Book 2**
> **Autumn's Touch – Book 3**
> **Winter's Flame – Book 4**

Elizabeth Rose

Prologue

Dying at the hands of his crew was not at all what Brody, Captain of the Sea Mirage, had planned for the day.

The swirling depths of the sea threatened to consume him. He stared down into the black water as he balanced precariously on a plank extending from the side of his ship. His mutinous crew, the cutthroat bunch of traitors, watched with bated breath as he teetered on the edge with his hands and feet tied by coarse rope.

Blast it all! This wasn't turning out to be a good day. He'd just recently inherited the title of Captain of the Sea Mirage when Rowen, one of the triplet bastards of King Edward III, abandoned his crew for the sake of a wench. Now, just as quickly as Brody had inherited his good fortune, it was about to be taken away.

"Go on – jump," demanded the rough voice of the oldest pirate on the ship, Old Man Muck. Having always held a grudge that he wasn't captain, Muck never stopped trying to make the Sea Mirage his. He was an angry man with a quick temper, no morals at all, and he never thought about anyone but himself. Aye, men like Muck were what gave pirates a bad reputation.

Muck poked Brody in the back with the tip of his sword, edging him forward. If Brody's hands and feet hadn't been tied, he'd take on Muck even without a weapon to save his ship. The Sea Mirage was the only home he had known for most his life. Unfortunately, these fickle pirates were also the only family he had now. Things couldn't possibly get any worse.

It was early morning as far as Brody could tell. The fog was thick, and he could barely see through the mist as they sailed into the white abyss.

"God's eyes, what's the matter with you, Muck?" spat Brody, turning his head to talk to the old man. "How did you and Lucky get aboard my ship in the first place? For that matter, how did you escape the dungeons of Hermitage Castle in Scotland after Rowen put you there to stay?"

Brody needed to stall for time and, hopefully, come up with a plan quickly. He'd been woken from a sound sleep by Muck and Lucky who must have come aboard at the last port before the ship set sail for the night.

He'd been dragged out of bed and removed from his cabin before he even knew what happened. Although he'd fought back, Muck and Lucky managed to tie him up and haul him to the side of the ship. His crew had done nothing at all to help him. Instead, they just stood and watched. Cowards! None of this made any sense.

"I told you, Rowen set us free," growled Muck, spittle dribbling down into his scraggly brown beard as he spoke. Muck's teeth were broken and rotten. His clothes were dirty and ripped. Brody could smell the stench emanating from the man's body all the way from the end of the plank.

"That's a lie," growled Brody. "Rowen is the one who put you two behind bars for attempting mutiny when the ship was under his command. He would never set you free."

"It was his brother, Reed, who let us out," admitted Lucky.

Muck shot him a menacing look, squinting his eyes as he spoke to his sidekick. "Shut your mouth, Lucky. I'm the one doing the talking, not you. Say another word, and I'll add to that scar on your neck."

"Sorry, Muck." Lucky rubbed the long scar across his neck that Rowen had given him years ago. His vocal chords had been cut, and Lucky was very lucky to be alive – hence it earned him the nickname. His voice suffered from the injury and sounded raspy and frightening when he spoke.

"I was right," said Brody. "Rowen didn't set you free. Crew, do you hear that?" He peered through the fog, his eyes traveling from Big Garth - his cook, over to Spider – the barrel-chested pirate with the hairy arms. Then his gaze settled on the tall pirate named Ash who walked with a limp. "Bid the devil, do something to help me instead of standing there watching!"

"I don't know," said the pirate named Odo. His eye nervously twitched as he studied Brody. "Old Man Muck does deserve to be cap'n."

"He's got a point there," said Spider. "Rowen deserted us, and now you won't even let us raid. Muck would never leave his ship for a woman. Neither would he keep us from raiding." The crew grew edgy as they discussed it.

"No matter if he deserted us, Rowen is no longer the captain of the Sea Mirage," Brody reminded them. "The ship is mine now."

"Not for long," said Muck.

The crew was anxious to raid once again, so they sided with Muck. The only crewmember that stayed loyal to Brody was the boy named Link. Link had been an orphan when Rowen took him onto the ship years ago as part of their dysfunctional family of less-than-honorable men.

"Leave Brody alone," shouted Link. "He's never done a thing to any of you." The boy was only four and ten years of age but had the courage of any of the seasoned men aboard the ship.

"Step back, boy, or you'll be walking the plank with him," warned Muck, swatting a bug at the back of his neck.

"Nay, I won't!" Link daringly pushed Muck. It was a foolish move on his part, but all the distraction Brody needed. With his feet still tied together, Brody hopped down to the deck, throwing his body at Muck. As he did, Muck turned around with his sword raised.

Using the blade to his advantage, Brody jabbed his arms upward, running the ropes that bound his wrists together, across the edge of the sword. He managed to cut his bindings and push away from the blade at the same time. Quickly, his nimble fingers removed the ropes from around his wrists. He dove for Muck, taking the old man down on the deck of the ship. The crew parted, watching the fight. They cheered and shouted. To them, this was naught more than a morning of entertainment.

Brody struggled with Muck, throwing a few punches. Two arms grabbed him from behind, and he turned to see Lucky helping the old man. With all the kicking and squirming, the ropes at Brody's ankles loosened. He reached down to free himself.

Seeing a dagger on the deck, he snatched it up. But when he stood, Muck was holding his blade to Link's throat.

"Reed might have told us not to kill you, but he never said a word about not killing the boy." Muck smirked, finding the leverage he needed. Link's brown eyes showed courage and also devotion to Brody. As much as Brody was itching to fight Muck, he wouldn't risk the boy's life.

"Nay! Let him go," said Brody.

"I agree, let the boy go," shouted Big Garth, coming

to Link's rescue. The crew moved in closer.

"If a single one of you makes a move, the boy is dead," warned Muck.

Lucky held up his sword, protecting Muck's back. "You heard him. Back off."

"What do you want?" asked Brody, hating the way the seedy pirate was using the life of the innocent boy for leverage.

"Jump overboard of your own accord, or the boy dies." Muck brought the blade closer to Link's throat and drew blood. "This ship is mine now."

"Nay!" Brody secretly slipped the dagger into the back of his breeches when they weren't watching. Then he held his hands up in the air. "Don't hurt him. Please." Link was like a younger brother to Brody. He didn't deserve to die. Brody did not doubt that Muck would kill Link if he didn't do as instructed.

"Don't make Brody jump," begged Link.

"There's an island nearby," said Muck. "If you can swim faster than the sharks, you might have a chance to make it there alive. Do it, and mayhap both of you will live."

"What do you say, Brody?" Lucky talked without looking back, still holding his sword up toward the crew.

Brody didn't have a chance in hell of beating Muck if his crew wasn't behind him. The crew had always been loyal to Rowen, but Muck had somehow convinced them to follow him instead. Then again, the pirates had known Muck longer. They had once been under the command of Muck's brother, One-Eyed Ron. Respect was something that had to be earned amongst pirates and thieves. Brody had lived with them for over ten years, but hadn't been captain long enough to earn their trust.

"All right. I'll do it," he agreed, seeing no other way out of the situation. "Just promise me you won't hurt the boy."

"I'll not make you any promises," grunted Muck. "But since I need a lackey aboard the ship, the boy won't be killed unless you give me trouble."

"I'm going." Brody nodded, looking out at the water. If only he could think of another plan. The end of the red cloth covering his hair blew in the breeze as he slowly made his way back down the plank, wanting to kill Muck for this. But Brody was one man against a crew that had turned mutinous. There was no hope for him or Link unless he followed Muck's command.

"Jump," ordered Muck from behind him.

Brody lined up his booted feet at the edge of the plank, feeling like he was going to his death. Could he swim to the island to save himself? He had an idea where they were, but in this fog, he couldn't be sure. How would he even know if he was swimming in the right direction? He looked down to the sea beneath him, not able to believe this was the way he would die. Water had always meant freedom to him, but now it was nothing more than a death sentence.

"Wait! Take this." Lucky used his foot and slid a goatskin across the plank to Brody.

"What are you giving him, you fool?" asked Muck.

"It's just some ale to help him survive if he happens to make it to the island," Lucky explained. Brody reached down and picked up the goatskin, slipping the strap over his shoulder.

"Do it!" shouted Muck. Link whimpered. When Brody glanced back, he saw more blood running from the boy's neck. His eyes scanned his crew members one by one, looking for someone who would have a change of heart. Not a one of them dared to make eye contact with him. Instead, they looked at the deck or off into the fog. Nay, none of them had a heart. He should have known better. His situation was hopeless.

"You won't get away with this Muck!" Brody promised. "I'll not only survive, but I swear I'll return and kill you for this. You'd better sleep with one eye open because the next shadow in the mist will be me, coming to slit your throat."

Then Brody turned around and dove into the water, only hoping there was an island nearby. If not, he'd never get the chance to kill Muck after all.

Chapter 1

Brody eyed the threatening sky as he tied off the last vine holding together his rough-crafted raft. He'd made the escape vessel from saplings and driftwood that he'd found on the deserted island after he was fortunate enough to make it to shore. Thankfully he'd had a dagger hidden in his waistbelt, or he wouldn't have even been able to make this.

He also had the goatskin filled with ale. Of course, the ale was long gone by now, even with the way he'd rationed it. Every time it rained, he collected rainwater to drink. He found some roots, acorns, brambles, roan berries and haw – the fruit of the hawthorn tree to eat. Still, the limited amount of food left him starving. He'd tried to fish, but without a net, he had little to no results.

Brody never thought he'd be stranded for so long or

he would have carved a notch in a tree for every day he'd been there. One day melded into the next, and he'd started getting dizzy and confused lately. He was no longer sure if he had been there a week or a month or possibly longer. With the fog they'd been having, sometimes he couldn't even tell if it was day or night. He had to get off of this island soon!

He thought for sure a passing ship would have rescued him by now. He'd been burning whatever he could find trying to make a signal fire high enough. Each day the sun would come out for a short while to dry the wood, but when the sun went down, it would rain all night, dousing whatever flame he had.

If he didn't get help soon, he might as well dig his own grave next.

Thunder rumbled overhead, not roiling him at all. Nothing seemed to bother him anymore. The driving force that kept him alive was the fact he wanted to live so that he could kill Muck. Now he understood Rowen's vengeance against the king all these years. Vengeance was a powerful motivator and gave men the will to survive to see justice done. No one was going to treat him this way and live to tell about it. He vowed he would kill Muck and then take back his ship if it was the last thing he ever did.

A movement on the water caught his attention, causing his head to snap upward. Straining his eyes, he was sure he could make out the silhouette of a passing ship in the mist. Could he use his raft and make it to the ship before it disappeared? Thunder rumbled again. With no choice but to try, he threw caution to the wind. Since he hadn't seen a passing ship the entire time he'd been here, this might be his only chance to get off this island.

He jumped up and ran to the shore, pulling his wooden raft behind him. Traipsing into the water with his shoes on, he positioned his raft and breathed a sigh of relief. This was it. He would be rescued from this hell today. He grabbed the homemade oars that were nothing more than branches with woven fronds on the ends. After placing them on the raft, he pushed the little raft out into deeper water. Then he raised a leg and climbed aboard. With the wind picking up from the approaching storm, he headed out to sea.

This was by no means the Sea Mirage, but the feeling of sailing on the water filled him with life. The winds picked up even more, and before he knew it, it started to rain.

He used an oar on first one side of the raft and then the other, trying not to lose sight of the ship in the distance. To his dismay, the ship he'd seen kept getting farther and farther away. He just couldn't catch it.

Why did he think they'd ever notice him when he was naught more than a speck on the vast sea? No one even knew he was there. At this rate, he'd never make it to the ship before it disappeared. Thinking of how he could move faster, he realized he had to use the wind to his advantage.

Using his oars, he tied them together with more spare vines. He then removed his white tunic and made a sail. Jamming the pole in between a few of the planks of the raft, he managed to erect a mast. Since he was experienced at sailing, he used his skills to make the wind work for him instead of against him. Before long, the ship was not only back in sight, but he was gaining speed.

The wind whipped against his face, mixed with rain that bit into his flesh. He held no pride of being the captain of an escape raft. Longing filled his soul to be back on his ship as captain of the Sea Mirage again.

Would Rowen ever find out what his old crew did to Brody? Brody would be sure to tell him if he ever made it back to the mainland alive.

The ship came into view, but fog was settling over the water making it hard to see. From what he could tell, it wasn't a large ship. It didn't look to be a cargo ship but rather a vessel used for fishing. It didn't matter. They could take him back to the mainland. He wasn't choosy at a time like this. Once he stepped foot on solid land again, he'd be able to hunt down and kill Old Man Muck.

The rain pelted down and a cold shiver ran up his spine.

The wind felt relentless against his body. He tried to tuck strands of hair back under his headscarf so he could keep a close eye on his target. He did all he could to hold on to the raft and sail it directly over to the fishing ship. But with the fog rising from the water even thicker than before, it made it hard to see. He had to catch the ship, or he was naught more than shark bait. This was his only chance to survive.

Gwendolen Fisher reeled in the fishing lines, trying to help secure her father's boat before the storm hit. Dressed in breeches and boots instead of a gown, and with her hair covered with a head cloth and hat, she fit right in with the rest of her father's crew.

Ever since the death of her mother, Gwen had wanted to stay as close to her father as possible. She was his only daughter and also his only child anymore as far as he was concerned. Her three older brothers, Aaron, Tristan, and Mardon, had left and no one knew where they went.

At one time her brothers had helped her father fish. Together, they'd sold their catches to townsfolk, merchants, and even nobles. It was a simple life, and they were far from wealthy, but the business kept food on the table and a roof over their heads.

As her brothers grew older, they had their minds set on so much more than just a handful of coins a week, or a boatload of smelly fish. One day they decided to go their own ways. They were looking for more in life than their father could ever give them.

They wanted fame, wealth, and excitement in their lives. Gwen only wanted her family together again – something she would never have.

"Gwen, get inside the cabin," called out her father, lifting a bottle of whisky to his lips. He'd started to partake of the drink right after her mother died. Cato Fisher was a proud man, and could not accept the fact he'd lost not only a wife but three strong, able-bodied sons as well. Nay, he was hardly ever sober anymore since he drank to ease the pain of losing so much. Her heart went out to him. She decided she would take the place of the sons he lost.

The sails whipped in the wind and cold rain fell from the heavens. The swells of the waves kept getting higher. Their little fishing ship was naught but a victim on the turbulent sea.

"I'm all right, Father," she yelled into the wind. "I'm just as capable as the rest of your crew. I want to help."

"Gwen, listen to him," shouted Leo, the eldest man of the crew. He was her father's age and also his best friend.

"Get off the deck before you're blown overboard," called out Flann, always being so bossy. Flann never liked the fact her father had brought her along on the fishing trips in the first place. The other two men tolerated Gwen and, at times, even treated her as if she were their daughter.

"I'm going to help, so we don't lose our catch." She yanked at one side of the net filled with fish, while the quietest of the crew, Gilroy, helped her to haul it aboard. Gwen was a small woman and hadn't the strength at seven and ten years of age to do the work of a mature man.

Although she tried her hardest, her fingers slipped. The ropes cut into her hands making her cry out. If she held on any longer, she risked losing a finger. Without another choice, she loosened her hold, and with it went the net as it fell back into the water. Her heart sank when she realized because of her; they'd just lost their entire catch of fish.

"Dammit, Gwen, I told you to let the men do that! Why don't you ever listen?" Her father tied the wheel to keep the ship on course and then hurriedly made his way across the wet deck toward her. His step wavered more from the drink than from the tossing of the ship. Still, he clutched the bottle of whisky in his hand, not willing to put it down. "Get below deck before I have to tie you to a mast," he growled.

"Nothing can stop me from helping, and you know it." Gwen looked over the rail to see the hoard of fish they'd caught swimming back out to sea. It was an unfortunate accident that would cost them a day's work. As she watched the turbulent sea take on a life of its own, the fog parted momentarily giving her a glimpse of something on the water.

Making her way closer to the rail, she held on tightly, straining her eyes to see what was floating toward the ship. It was dark and mysterious and almost looked like a man aboard a raft. "Father, Look! I think it's a man." She pointed anxiously to the object, eager to share her find. Her father didn't look. Instead, he reached out and yanked her away from the sidewall.

"If you don't start listening to me, I'm going to leave you ashore next time." He dragged her toward the hatch that led to the bowels of the ship.

"Nay, there's something there I tell you," she said again. Before her father could ignore her a second time, someone called to them from down in the water.

"Ahoy! Can you hear me?"

"What was that?" Flann stood up straight, his eyes darting back and forth. "I think my ears are playing tricks on me in this storm."

"I heard it too. It sounded like a voice," surmised Gilroy.

"It's a man, I tell you. A man on a raft." Gwen broke free of her father's hold and ran across the deck. She slipped and almost ended up falling over the edge. After making it to the rail, she held on tightly and called out to the man in the fog.

"We hear you. Do you need help?" She waved one arm over her head.

"Of course, he needs help," spat Flann, pushing her aside. "Leo, give me a hand pulling him aboard."

Gwen shivered in her wet clothes as she watched the men pull the drifter aboard. From the foggy mist emerged a bare-chested god of the sea. He wore a red headscarf over long, black hair. A dark, short beard and mustache outlined his pear-shaped face. He was soaked from the storm. His broad chest looked hard, and so did his nipples. He had to be freezing in the cold weather, especially since he was dripping wet. How had he come to be out on the sea all alone?

The crew reached down to help him. The mysterious man took a white tunic off a tall pole on the raft and extended his free hand to Leo. When his feet hit the deck of the ship, she could see he wasn't as tall as her father's crew. Still, he held an air of confidence about him. Dark brown eyes looked over from under thick brows. He seemed to be in his early twenties.

"What happened to you?" asked her father, rushing over to join them.

"Thank you for helping me," said the man, relief echoing in his words. His skin looked tanned, and there were dark circles under his eyes. She wondered if he was ill. His thin lips were dry and cracked from the elements. He probably hadn't had fresh water in a long time. As she surveyed him even closer, she realized his body shook slightly.

"You're shivering," she said, causing the man to look right into her eyes this time. In the round, brown depths of his orbs hung a hint of sadness that couldn't be masked. This man had been through something horrible, she was sure of it. She longed to find out more.

"You're a wench," he said in astonishment. He donned the white tunic over his head without even wavering on the rocky ship. That told her he was used to being on the sea.

"I'm not a wench – I'm a girl," she retorted, sad to see him don his shirt and block her view of his enticing naked chest.

"This is my daughter, Gwendolen," said her father. "I'm Cato Fisher. This is my crew, Leo, Gilroy, and Flann."

"Thank you, once again," said the man, being ever so polite. "My name is Brody."

"Where's your ship?" asked Flann.

"Did you have an accident at sea?" asked Leo.

"You could say that," he answered. A shadow crossed his face. "I'm afraid I'm now a captain without a ship. However, I hope to recover the Sea Mirage again someday soon."

"Sea Mirage?" Gwen's father's spine stiffened, and so did his grip on the bottle. "I've heard of that ship. It's said to be the fastest ship on the sea."

"Aye. That would be the one." Brody smiled slightly, nodding his head proudly.

"It's also said to be a pirate ship," growled her father. He turned his head and spat on the deck in disgust.

Gwen gasped. Was this man a pirate? Pirates upset her father. So much so, that she knew this man's presence here was going to end up being a bad situation. Brody's dark gaze skimmed over her before returning to her father.

"I'm trying to get to Whitehaven," he said. "Can you help me?"

"Whitehaven?" asked Flann. "We're going to Cornwall."

"Then I'm thankful for anywhere you can take me that is dry land. On the mainland," he added as an afterthought, making Gwen wonder if he'd been on an island recently.

"No time for talk," said her father. His eyes bore into Brody. Disgust and anger washed over his face. "This storm doesn't look to be letting up. We need all the help we can get. Are you in any condition to work? We need to secure our ship."

"Aye, of course," Brody said with a nod of his head. "I'd be more than happy to help. It's the least I can do." He headed to the other side of the ship to grab a loose line flapping in the breeze.

"Gwen. Men," her father said under his breath, his eyes never leaving Brody. "Be careful. He's a bloody pirate and can't be trusted."

"A pirate?" Gwen asked, speaking a bit too loud. The man named Brody lifted his face as he worked, watching from the sides of his eyes.

"Shall we get rid of him?" mumbled Flann. His hands balled into fists. Flann couldn't be trusted either. Gwen did not doubt that if her father wanted Brody gone, Flann would strangle him with his bare hands if need be.

"He'll never know what hit him." Leo's hand covered the hilt of his long fishing knife at his waist.

"Nay. Not yet," said her father, eyeing up the man

and then the sky. "We'll let him help get us through this storm first. Then we'll dump him back into the sea where cutthroats like him belong. I'm sure there was a damned good reason why he was out there in the first place. Just watch your backs. All of you. I don't like him being aboard the ship."

"How can you talk about him like that when you don't even know him?" asked Gwen.

"You stay away from that pirate," her father warned her, his teeth gritting as he spoke. "Do you hear me, Daughter? Men like him want one thing only."

"To rob us?" she asked with a cocky smile, knowing what he meant, but ignoring her father's warning.

"To rob young girls like you of something you will never be able to replace." Cato lifted the bottle to his lips and took a long draw.

The boat relentlessly rocked back and forth in the wind. Even with the amount of alcohol in him, her father managed to maintain his sea legs about him. Gwen held on for dear life. Storms frightened her. Even more than pirates.

"You need to shorten the sail," the pirate called out from the opposite side of the deck. His face turned upward. He surveyed the large square sail filled with air. In the strong wind, it was ready to burst.

"It's too dangerous at this point," said Cato. "The lines are tangled up near the top. I'm not going to risk the lives of my men asking them to climb the rigging in the storm to fix it."

"I'll do it," offered the man named Brody. Before Gwen knew what was happening, the pirate was climbing the rigging like a monkey with his dagger clenched between his teeth.

The ship tossed back and forth in the high waves, taking massive amounts of water on deck. The full sail billowed out, pushing the boat across the turbulent sea much too quickly.

"We're going to capsize," Gilroy shouted into the wind. Gwen could feel his fear. The ship had never leaned so far to the side as it was now. It did look like they'd capsize. Fear coursed through her and she wished they were all safely back on land.

"Man your stations. Now!" yelled her father.

"Gwen, get below deck," scolded Leo as he hurried past her, trying to make his way to the bow.

"I'm going," she said, feeling sick to her stomach. Lightning slashed across the darkened sky, and thunder reverberated in her chest. This was the worst storm she'd ever been in, and it frightened her worse than any of her nightmares. It was a night just like this when her mother passed away. Storms had terrified her ever since. Her father knew it and had tried to keep her close. That's why he'd been so protective of her through the years. Her brothers used to watch over her as well, being older than her. She missed them and never understood why her father had never gone after them and brought them home. They'd left in a storm one night. Aye, she hated storms in more ways than one.

She looked up to see Brody above them, shortening the sail, which miraculously managed to slow down their travels. If not for him, their boat would have broken apart in the storm. He was on his way back down to the deck when a huge swell hit the side of the ship. She held her breath as water sloshed over the sidewall and covered her head. The wave crashed upward into the rigging hitting Brody full force.

"Nay!" she cried out as she saw him lose his footing, only holding on by one hand from a loose line. "He's going to fall," she called out to the others. "Someone, save him."

"We can't," answered Leo, trying to secure the rest of the lines and fishing equipment before it was all washed overboard. "We have all we can do to save the ship. Now get to safety, Gwen. Hurry."

"Father, help him," she called out, holding on to things to try to make her way to the pirate without falling. Her father was having a hard time steering the ship and just shook his head.

"He's a pirate, Gwen. Just let him go."

"Nay! How can you say that? He just risked his life to help us." Without another word, she turned and ran to the rigging, holding tightly to the lines as she started to climb, trying to help him. If no one else cared about the man's life – she did. No matter if he was a pirate or a king, he deserved to be helped since he'd risked his life to save them.

"Go down, sweetheart," she heard Brody call out to her. "This is no place for a lady."

"Nay. I'm going to help you." She liked the fact he'd called her a lady, not to mention sweetheart. No one had ever done that before. She was naught but the daughter of a poor fisherman. Plus, she dressed and acted like a boy. Sometimes, she thought even her father considered her a boy. Or perhaps, he only wished she was one of the sons he'd lost. But she could never replace her brothers, even as hard as she tried to fill that void. She'd always wanted to ease her father's pain and make him happy again - the way he used to be so many years ago. If only she'd been born a boy, perhaps her father wouldn't have taken to the bottle so hard.

She neared Brody, but by the time she did, he'd managed to secure himself in the rigging. The cold wind blew against her wet clothes, and she shook like a leaf on a tree.

The man's tunic was torn open, flapping around him in the wicked wind. She couldn't even imagine how cold he felt. Then a flash of lightning split the sky, and simultaneously she heard a deafening noise. The hair on her arms stood on end, making her feel numb. Lightning had just struck the main mast!

"Gwen!" cried out one of the crew, but she could barely hear him since there was such a loud pounding in her ears. Was it the sound of her heartbeat and the blood rushing through her body? Was she going to die?

Her head dizzied and her grip loosened on the lines. Then the ship listed hard to port. She heard the sound of splintering wood above her. To her horror, the main mast was falling – with her on it.

"Help!" she cried out, tumbling toward the water. It was almost as if it happened in slow motion as her body, as well as the broken mast, fell toward the angry sea. Her life flashed before her eyes.

Brody had managed to drop to safety and was standing atop the sidewall. Her gaze met his when she fell past him, silently begging for his help, but no longer able to speak. The last thing she remembered before being covered by the turbulent black waters was Brody diving into the sea after her.

Chapter 2

Gwen was having a horrible dream and wanted to wake up. She felt the weight of the world pressing against her chest, and could barely breathe. It made her wonder if she were trapped under the broken mast of the ship. Thankfully, she wasn't under water. Still, the taste of salt water burned the back of her throat and made her eyes sting. The sound of gulls screeching from above her, intermingled with the lapping rhythm of the waves hitting the shore.

She needed to wake up from this horrible nightmare. Something warmed her face, and a bright light burned the insides of her closed lids. Slowly, she opened one eye and then the other. Seeing the sun and a blue sky above her, she realized she was in a prone position. The awful weight on her chest made her look down toward her feet. When she did, she screamed. The pirate was on top of her!

"What is it? Why did you scream?" His head lifted. Big brown eyes stared into hers as his long, loose hair spanned out around him and lifted in the breeze. "Are you all right, sweetheart?"

He'd used the endearment with her more than once now. She liked it, but it wasn't proper since she didn't even know him. Although he seemed like a nice enough man, her father warned her to stay away from him. Of course, she didn't have a choice in this situation. It all came back to her clearly now. She fell overboard in the storm. Then, the pirate named Brody jumped in the sea to save her.

"Get off of me," she retorted, trying to push his weight from her body. He sat up. She followed his action, but the rocking made her fall against him. They seemed to be on a raft or perhaps a piece of wreckage. The movement of their bodies made the raft tilt. His arms closed around her protectively. Even though they were both wet, she felt his body heat between them. Never before had she been in such a precarious position with a man.

"Don't move so quickly or you're going to dump us back into the sea," he warned, his voice sounding rugged and deep.

"Where's my father's ship?" she asked, her eyes darting around, scoping the water. "Where are my father and the crew?" Terror-stricken, she realized she was alone with the pirate.

"We lost them in the storm," he explained, not letting loose of his hold on her. "The mast was struck by lightning, and you fell into the sea. I jumped in after you. Don't you remember?"

She did remember. Only too well. She also realized that she was alone with this man, and no one was going to come to her rescue.

"You – you saved me," she said feeling grateful and frightened all at the same time.

"Aye." He nodded his head. The blue sky above them almost seemed to make his eyes twinkle. A pirate's eyes wouldn't twinkle, would they?

"Why did you risk your life and jump into the water after me? You don't even know me."

"Unlike some of us who judge a man before they know him, I have no qualms about saving a maiden in distress – no questions asked."

"Thank you." She relaxed slightly in his arms, her back pressed up against his chest. His kindness was intoxicating. "Where are we?"

"I can see the coast from here, so thankfully, we haven't drifted out to sea. It looks like Cornwall if I'm not mistaken."

"Cornwall? How can that be?" She squinted in the sun, staring at the rocky coastline. "We were fishing near the Isle of Man, which is far from Cornwall."

"The wind must have blown us here," he told her. "We've been at sea since yesterday."

"That long?" She made the mistake of moving too

quickly. Water sloshed up on the small raft that was meant for one. She almost lost her balance, but Brody kept her secure.

"You've been through a lot," he told her. "You were shivering from the cold, so I pressed my body up against yours to keep you warm. The sun has dried our clothes partially. Here, have some water." He held up what looked like a goatskin filled with liquid to her lips.

"Where did you get this?" Her shaking hands reached out for it.

"Drink." He held it while she took a sip. The water tasted cold and refreshing.

"Thank you. Now tell me where you got fresh water."

"It's the last of the rain water I collected while I was on the island. I had the goatskin when I left the Sea Mirage."

"Sea Mirage?" She looked up, shading her eyes from the sun. "Oh, that's right. It's your pirate ship. So, where is it?"

Brody had said too much. He'd mentioned his ship again, and now the girl was asking questions he didn't want to answer. It had been bad enough when he'd accidentally mentioned it in front of her father. Because of it, Brody overheard her father saying he was going to dump him back into the sea because he was a pirate. The less she knew about him, the better. He needed to get back to Whitehaven quickly and talk to Rowen about everything that had happened. That's all that mattered to him. He'd get everything else sorted out later.

The whole incident aboard the Sea Mirage still gnawed at his gut. Muck was lying, and he needed to learn the truth. The only problem was, the storm had blown them to kingdom come. They were nowhere near Whitehaven anymore. It was his assumption, by the look of the rocky coast, that they were nearing Cornwall at the southern tip of England.

Brody groaned and rubbed his leg. His flesh had broken open on a piece of flotsam when he'd jumped into the water to save Gwen. He'd managed to stop the bleeding by tying his headscarf around the wound, but his leg hurt like the devil. He wasn't at all sure he could even stand. God's eyes, he hoped it wasn't becoming infected.

"You're hurt," she said, eying his wound. "And you're bleeding."

"It's nothing," he said, trying to play it off. He didn't need a wench in a frenzy to add to the rest of his problems. He had to keep her calm.

"I'm not daft." She removed her headscarf and, to his surprise, long bouncing blond curls spilled out, reminding him she was a girl. "I'm going to use this to change the bloody wrapping on your leg. I only wish I hadn't lost my hat, as it could have shaded me from the sun."

"I'm fine," he told her.

"You are not fine. Now let me do it." With gentle and nimble fingers, she unwrapped the bloody binding, inspecting his wound. Her sparkling eyes narrowed, and she shook her head. "Give me some of that water so I can cleanse the wound." Her hand reached out, but her attention stayed on his leg.

"Nay. We've only got a small amount of fresh water left," he told her, cradling the goatskin to his chest like a baby. "We need to save it until we are sure we can find more."

"There's the coast, so we don't need to worry. We'll have plenty of fresh water soon."

What was happening here? He thought he was the one comforting her when, in reality, it was the opposite way around now. Gwen looked to be young but seemed more mature when she tried to comfort him. He hadn't had anyone other than Rowen who cared for him since the day he was abducted by pirates. It felt nice.

"We're drifting into the area of the St. Agnes caves," he told her, knowing the area well as this is where he'd lived before he'd become a pirate. "It is rocky and desolate here. It might take us days to get back to civilization. I'm not even sure if I can stand on my leg."

"Then I'll wrap it for now, but I'll clean it as soon as we get ashore." She finished wrapping his leg with the cloth.

Sure enough, their raft drifted toward the caves just like he knew it would.

Gwen watched in awe as they drifted closer to the St. Agnes caves. "It is said that these caves are inhabited by giants and mermaids and other creatures," she told him, feeling apprehensive to be so close.

He chuckled. "That is naught but a legend, my dear. Obviously made up by some greedy pirate to keep everyone out of the caves and away from his booty."

"I've always been intrigued by the caves, but my father warned me never to go in them."

"He also warned you to stay away from me, but as you can see – I'm harmless."

"Are you?" She wrapped her arms around herself, not sure what to think. "You could be trying to gain my trust so you can have your way with me later."

"If I wanted you, I wouldn't waste time with trying to gain your trust. After all, I'm a pirate. That's what pirate's do – take what they want."

She wasn't sure if he was serious or trying to scare her. She decided not to talk to him so much and also to keep her distance. Hopefully, with his bad leg, she could outrun him and get to safety as soon as they hit the shore.

"I'll get off first and make certain everything's safe," he told her as they drifted closer to the cave.

The water didn't look deep at all. Gwen was excited and fascinated by the caves as well as a little scared. She felt daring being in this area and with a dangerous pirate at her side. Why did it make her feel so alive?

She could no longer wait. In one motion, she swung her feet over the edge of the raft, preparing to disembark. When she did, it caused the raft to become unbalanced, and they were both dumped into the water. Breaking the surface, she gasped for breath, getting her footing. It was a little deeper than she'd thought.

"Bid the devil," she heard Brody cry out. When he stood, the water was up to his waist.

She smiled. "Sorry about that."

"What's one more dip in the sea?" he grumbled, pulling the raft up to the rocky shore. His strong, glistening wet chest gleamed in the sunshine. It was hard for her to look away. This man intrigued her just as much as the caves.

Water trickled into several of the caves. Over the rocks, further down, there was a beach in the far distance. Shading her eyes, Gwen surveyed that she could almost see the docks. She had planned to run, but when she glanced back at Brody, she decided he didn't seem that threatening after all. By the looks of his leg, even if he tried something with her she'd still be able to get away. Nay, he saved her life and so she would help him.

"If we hurry, we might be able to walk down the beach and get to the docks by sunset," she told him. "I know where we are now. I'm familiar with this area. This is where my father sometimes brings his catch to sell or trade."

"I know the area too," he told her.

"My father does business in some of the towns around St. Agnes. We usually dock just down the beach. There is a tavern not far from here. My father goes there at times to get something to eat."

"Or drink," he mumbled, tying up the raft. It was no secret he was referring to her father's fondness of the bottle. Not wanting to speak ill of her father, she pretended not to hear him.

"How do you know these caves?" she asked, scanning the area, feeling a shiver go through her body. "I suppose you've got booty hidden inside?"

"Hah! If that were true, I'd be running to get it, even with a bad leg."

"So, you have sailed here before with your crew?"

He looked up but didn't respond. He seemed to be remembering something but wasn't in a hurry to share it with her.

"Mayhap my father has already made it to shore with his crew," she suggested, trying to be optimistic. "Let's go see." Taking off at a brisk pace, she hurried over the rocks, anxious to find them. But when she heard Brody groan, she stopped and turned around. He was struggling to walk, grimacing with every step he took. The water around his leg turned a bright red. He'd started bleeding again. She wasn't even sure his leg wasn't broken or sprained. Her heart went out to him.

"Here, let me help." Being no stranger to physical work, she rushed over to him and slipped her arm around him. "Lean on me."

"I won't be helped by a wench!" His body stiffened.

"Have it your way." She dropped her arm from around him. "Your face looks pale. Are you ill?"

"I'm wounded, not to mention I have almost drowned twice lately. I've had very little fresh water to drink and barely anything to eat. So, what do you think?"

She felt as if he'd scolded her. She didn't like it, even if she felt sorry for the man. "There's no reason to become curt with me. We've both had some bad times lately, so I'd appreciate if you didn't try to make me feel daft or guilty again."

He stood up straight with a jerk, and his eyes bore into her. "No lady speaks to a man in that manner. Especially not to a pirate! You play with fire and are going to get burned someday."

Gwen had been acting more like a boy most her life, so it came naturally to her to boldly speak her mind. She didn't know how to act like a lady and wasn't going to start now. "Mayhap I can pull you on the raft," she suggested. "Since you are wounded, it would be faster to travel in the water."

"For a girl who says she knows this area, you're forgetting a few things." He groaned again and sat on a rock, touching his leg with his fingertips, testing the wound. He grimaced when his finger poked at his leg, which told her he was in dire pain. "This time of year, the sun goes down quickly. It'll make it harder to travel over the rocky ground in the dark. And when the tide comes in we'll have to make our way to higher ground."

"So, you're saying we're not going to try to find my father and his crew after all?"

"Nay. Not today." He removed his binding and inspected his wound.

She let out an exasperated breath. They were so close to the docks and finding help. "There's still light left. If we hurry, we could make it to the docks before the tide comes in. We need to try."

"Then go," he said, not even looking at her when he spoke. "No one is asking you to stay."

"Stay?" She hadn't even considered the thought, but he obviously had. She glanced at Brody, and then her eyes darted over to the caves. While both intrigued her, she didn't want to be alone in the dark with either of them. "If I leave you, where will you go tonight? What will you do? You can barely walk. And you're bleeding."

"That's right, I am," he said, still not looking at her when he spoke. "But I'm naught more than a cutthroat, so you don't need to worry about me. Just throw me back in the sea where all pirates belong. After all, that's what your father would do, wouldn't he?" With his head still down, his eyes lifted to meet hers. He looked dangerous and angry. It caused a chill to run up her spine.

"Oh. You heard him," she remarked softly, feeling embarrassed that he'd overheard their conversation on the ship. She hoped he wouldn't be upset and take it out on her now. Feeling restless and not knowing what else to say, she picked up the edge of her tunic and wrung out the water. She contemplated running now, but for some reason, she stayed.

"Pirates have bloody good ears, sweetheart." He tied the cloth back around his leg and stood. He took a step and winced. Even through the pain, he continued to walk toward her.

How could she leave him now? He could have been safe aboard the fishing ship, but instead, he chose to dive into the water to save her life. She supposed she owed him a favor. With one last glance over her shoulder, she looked down the beach, wanting to go, but at the same time feeling as if she needed to stay. She sighed and turned back to him.

"Let me help." She tried once more. She put her arm around him again. This time he didn't stop her. He leaned against her as they made their way toward the caves.

"I'm not used to being helped by a lady." He didn't sound so repelled at the idea this time. The low timbre of his voice was rich and masculine. It matched the very handsome man. She felt as if he were trying to be polite since he hadn't called her a wench again.

"Well, I'm not used to being called a lady," she admitted flashing a quick smile.

"Would you rather I stick to wench?"

"Nay," she blurted out. "Please, don't."

When he chuckled, she realized he'd only been jesting.

Thunder rumbled in the distance as black clouds rolled in overhead. With it went any warmth from the sun.

"Not more rain," he protested.

"We can find shelter in the caves," she told him, heading to the one closest to them.

"If we don't get warm and dry we might not be alive on the morrow."

"When will the tide come in?" she asked. It started to drizzle.

He stopped and looked up at the moon, still partially visible in the daytime sky. "By my calculations, we should have at least a few good hours before the tide comes in. We can stay here for a while. We'll try to get to higher ground as soon as it stops raining."

"Then let's get inside and out of the rain."

Brody let the girl help him into the cave. Usually, he wouldn't accept help from a woman, but his ordeal and his wound were taking a toll on him. He was tired and drained of energy. He was also to the point that he didn't even feel hungry anymore since it had been so long since he'd had a real meal. His throat felt parched, and with the pain in his leg, all he wanted was a bottle of rum right now. Hating to accept her help, he'd agreed because she was the only one here to do it. He also didn't want her wandering off on her own, and not being able to protect her. Aye, he was glad she decided to stay.

They made their way to the first cave where they would have shelter from the rain. She stopped in the entranceway, hesitant to go inside.

"What's wrong?" he asked her. "Afraid the giants will eat you in your sleep? Or perhaps that the mermaids will curse you?" He chuckled, stopping behind her.

"It is very dark in there. Perhaps we should stay at the mouth of the cave where it's still light. I wouldn't want to run into any critters hiding deep inside the cave."

"Great idea," he said, not caring in the least. He hobbled into the cave and sat down in the shadows. It was cool and damp inside, but at least they were out of the wind and rain.

"So, this is the cave." She stood there for a moment, letting her eyes get used to the last bit of light that bathed the cave entrance only. Her sweet voice echoed off the walls as she ventured inside slowly, acting as if it were a place to be reverent.

"Aye, it is a cave," he answered.

"Not just any cave," she said, taking a step inside. "I've heard legends that these caves are magical. Lovers hid here many years ago before tragedy took their lives. It is said to enter the lovers' caves will ensure two people will fall in love. Supposedly, if you touch the wall, you can feel the love shared by the legendary lovers that once hid here."

"I don't believe in that kind of nonsense."

Cautiously, she stepped forward, daring to reach out her fingers to touch the cave wall. "Are you saying you don't believe in legends or that you don't believe in falling in love?"

"Neither," he said, just being honest. Her head snapped around to look at him. Although her face was in shadow, it was evident she was scowling at him right now. Just his luck to be stranded with a woman who dressed and acted like a boy yet had her head filled with fantasies of legends and falling in love. This girl was very complicated.

"How can you say that?" she asked, sounding as if his answer displeased her.

"It's all nonsense. The legend is only a story made up, probably by a man to get a wench into bed with him. And the only people who touch these walls are young fools on a dare. They come here at night to prove nothing scares them, carving their names into the stone only to have their lives destroyed afterward because of it."

Gwen felt a tingle run up her spine and a heat engulf her as she laid her entire hand on the cave wall next. She wondered if it was just the excitement of being here or if these caves really held some sort of magic. Was she being silly to believe in ancient legends? And was she a fool for believing in love?

Brody seemed to think so. "You don't know what you're saying."

"Oh, but I assure you, I do," said Brody. "I know from experience."

"Experience?" Her hand stilled on the wall, and she looked over her shoulder at him. "What do you mean?"

"Years ago, I was one of those fools on a dare that sneaked into the cave and etched my name into the stone."

He walked up next to her and reached up higher on the wall. With the tip of his finger, he traced letters carved into the stone that she hadn't even noticed were there. Sure enough, the name Brody was scratched into the cave wall in big, bold letters. How hadn't she seen this?

"You – you're telling the truth."

He turned his head to look at her. His eyes were dark, dangerous and sultry. The daylight from behind him at the cave opening illuminated the outline of his body. "Of course I am. Why do you sound so surprised? Is it because I'm a pirate and to you, all pirates are naught but thieves and liars?"

Something came alive inside her with every swipe of his finger against the outline of his name in the stone. He touched the wall of the cave as if he was caressing a lover. Somehow, she felt it as if he were touching her. Was it just her imagination? Her heart pounded in her ears, mixed with the sound of the waves lapping against the rocks outside the cave. The waves pushed forward and then retreated, like a secret lover in the night. All she could think about was the fact she was in the lovers' cave . . . alone . . . with a very handsome pirate. She squeezed her eyes closed, feeling confusion cloud her head.

"Are you ill?" His hot breath in her ear caused her to jump backward. Her eyes sprang open, and she broke the connection of whatever it was she'd been feeling between them. She quickly stepped away from the wall, suddenly feeling very foolish. It had to be the legend of the lovers that made her feel a spark between them. Still, she needed to know if he felt anything at all.

"We touched the wall at the same time," she said, no louder than a whisper.

"And now you think we'll fall madly in love?" His deep laughter echoed off the walls of the cave. "That is the most ridiculous thing I've ever heard. Now, come over here and put your arm around me."

"What?" she blurted out, wondering if he'd felt all hot and flushed like her.

"I need you to help me walk."

"Oh. Of course." Part of her wanted him to touch her the way he'd touched the wall. Thoughts of sensuality rushed through her. It had to be just her imagination. It was silly, just like he said.

"You're cold," he said when she slipped her arm around him. "I'll warm you."

"Nay, I'm not cold." Her teeth chattered as if on cue to call her a liar.

"Your words say one thing yet your body says something else."

She was cold – yet hot at the same time. She couldn't explain it, so didn't bother to try.

"You're shivering," he continued.

She was shaking, but it wasn't from the weather. It was because of what she'd felt between them, and that scared her. Had something happened when they both touched the wall at the same time? And could the legend be true after all?

Anxious and confused, she wasn't sure what to think. Then Brody reached out for her. Her eyes closed as he wrapped his arms around her in a protective hold.

"Everything will work out," he whispered, rubbing his cheek against her hair. "We'll find your father, don't worry."

"I hope so." She felt the urge to look up into his eyes, needing to know if he felt attracted to her at all. "Don't you feel it?" she asked, wetting her dry lips with her tongue.

"Feel what?" He looked down, his focus on her mouth if she wasn't mistaken.

"We touched the wall at the same time. Something happened between us. I felt it."

"The last time I touched that bloody wall, I was captured by pirates," he scoffed. "These walls are nothing but a curse. I haven't been back to Cornwall for over ten years and have no desire to be here now."

"You – were captured by pirates?"

"Aye. You see, I wasn't always a pirate, Gwen."

He'd used her name, and she liked it. Curious, she found herself needing to know more. "Please, continue," she told him. "I'd like to hear about how you became a pirate."

He hesitated, and for a moment she didn't think he would. But then he opened up a part of his life to her after all.

"I was here with my good friend, Edwin, on a dare. It was right after I lost my family to a passing pestilence. Edwin's family felt sorry for me and took me in. Besides them, I was always treated by everyone else as an orphan."

"I'm so sorry. I didn't know." Her gaze dropped to his mouth. They were standing very close. It would be so easy to kiss him. His head lowered, and his face came closer.

"I wasn't always a pirate. At one time I was a son of a fisherman and no different than you."

"Didn't anyone come looking for you?"

"Who would come looking for an orphan? My family was gone, and I hadn't made many friends since I was aboard the ship and at sea most the time."

"You were part of your father's crew, just like me."

His head bobbed up and down in agreement.

"What about your friend, Edwin?" she asked. "What happened to him?"

"I don't know. The pirates had captured him at first. I fought them off, and told Edwin to run and get help. I thought he'd be back with his father and some of the men from the village. Mayhap they did return, but I never had the chance to find out. I was scooped up and thrown onto the Sea Mirage by the infamous captain, One-Eyed Ron. From that day on . . . I was considered his property. And a pirate."

"That's awful," she said, her heart going out to him. She faced him and slipped her arms around his waist, just trying to get warm. Her teeth chattered so much they rattled her brain. If she had been thinking with a sound mind, she would have never been so bold.

His hand gently cupped and lifted her chin, bringing her mouth closer to his. Then he dipped down, and their lips touched – and she let him do it. Heat seared through her as they shared a kiss. He tasted like fresh air mixed with the salty sea. Dangerous, yet exciting. His hand reached out, and he cupped her cheek next. Tilting her head toward him, she leaned into his caress as her eyes drifted closed. She reveled in the feel of his warmth against her skin.

Aye, there was something between them, and he could not deny it. He had felt it, too. She was sure of it. Why else would he kiss her?

"We both touched the wall, and look what happened," she said, just to prove her point about believing in legends. "Do you see what I mean?"

He hesitated for a moment, causing her to open her eyes. Then he cleared his throat before he spoke. "I've had a change of mind." His arms fell from around her body as he released her. With it went the excitement and heat she'd felt between them. Then he turned away, staring at his carved name on the wall as he talked. "This place holds bad memories for me, and I don't want to stay here any longer."

"You don't?" This wasn't what she wanted to hear. She thought for sure he'd say he felt something, too. That now, after touching the wall at the same time, they were falling in love. But instead, he said the opposite.

"Perhaps we can make it down the beach before the tide comes in after all. No sense waiting any longer. Let's get out of this god-forsaken cave and go find some warm shelter, food, and ale for the night."

He limped out of the cave, leaving her standing there alone. She looked over to the wall and sadly shook her head. Now, it just seemed to be a cursed wall like he said. Brody's name was scratched into the stone in tall letters, reminding everyone that he'd been there. She thought of his sad story. There was no love here. What she'd felt was naught more than her imagination. But now, that was gone, too. Mayhap he was right. This cave was nothing but the product of an ill legend devised by pirates to lure young people away from their families. A shiver coursed through her.

"Aye, let's get out of here and never look back," she told him, pushing past him and leading the way.

Chapter 3

Brody's leg hurt like hell and all he wanted to do was sit down, but he had to keep going. The tide was already starting to come in, making it hard to walk in the water. A better idea would have been to stay put somewhere until morning. However, after touching that blasted wall, he couldn't stop thinking about the legends Gwen mentioned.

Was it just the power of suggestion that made him kiss her? He'd had the overwhelming urge to press his lips against hers. And before he could talk himself out of it – he kissed her. It felt so good that now he wished he had never given in to his impulses. He did feel something for Gwen, but what did it matter? They could never end up together.

After all, he was just a pirate, and she was the daughter of a fisherman who wanted to take off every bloody pirate's head. Brody couldn't blame her father for feeling this way. He only wanted the best for his daughter. Gwen might dress and act like a boy, but that kiss told him that she was a diamond in the rough.

Just thinking about the kiss they'd shared made his lips tingle. It was the oddest thing. Then when he'd pulled Gwen into his arms, he felt as if he'd known her forever. He didn't quite understand it. Mayhap, he was just feeling randy since he'd been living at sea and hadn't had a proper bedding in some time now.

He watched Gwen walking in front of him - the last rays of sunset casting a golden glow over her body. With her long, blond curls released from their confinement, her hair bounced back and forth with every step she took. She was an angel in disguise.

Gwen couldn't hide her girly figure beneath her male attire. His eyes focused on her tiny waist and the delectable roundness of her bottom end. He'd felt her feminine curves when he'd pulled her into his arms. The swells of her breasts pushed up against his chest had made him excited. He shook his head, trying to clear his thoughts. All he could think about now was bedding her. It was only lust, he reminded himself. She was a young woman, and he wouldn't roger her at the rail like most of his crew would have had no qualms in doing. Nay, he needed to concentrate on finding a place to stay and healing his leg. All other thoughts, he needed to push from his mind.

Gwen stopped in her tracks causing him to walk into her. He reached out and steadied her from falling.

Or, mayhap, it was to keep himself from hitting the ground. After being almost drowned twice lately and not having enough fresh water or food, his body was breaking down. He could no longer think with a clear head. He felt dizzy and his leg throbbed. He needed to find somewhere to sit down before he fell over.

"Sorry," she said, looking back over her shoulder with those big, beautiful eyes. So innocent, yet at the same time filled with courage and vigor. "I didn't mean to stop so quickly, but I was wondering if we should move to higher land. The tide is coming in fast. I'm not sure if we'll make it all the way to the docks before we're swept out to sea."

"We won't," he told her, knowing all along it wasn't a good idea. If he hadn't been in such a hurry to get out of the cave and away from his bad memories, he would have thought of another plan. He looked up the embankment, recognizing this rocky ground. "We'll go up there," he told her. "Just atop the hill, there is a place called the Three Gulls Inn. That's where we'll spend the night."

She strained her eyes to see the area, nodding in agreement. "Yes, I remember that inn. It has a tavern inside. My father and brothers used to go there every time they came back from a fishing trip. My mother used to warn me not to go inside. I snuck in once and saw my father and brothers drinking with a bunch of men. The men all wore red head cloths, ragged clothes, and some had black hats. They scared me. They all carried swords. They also had wooden chests filled with coins that they were counting. My father and brothers were doing it as well."

"Sounds like pirates to me."

"Don't say that." She headed up the embankment and he followed. "You think everyone is a pirate or has some dealing with one."

"It is possible."

She stopped in her tracks and turned around. "What's possible?"

"That your father and brothers had dealings with pirates. It's no secret that the coasts of Cornwall are filled with them."

"I don't want to ever hear anything like that again about my father and brothers. Do you understand, Brody – Brody . . . what is your surname, anyway?"

"I don't know," he told her. "No one ever used surnames when I was a child. I don't think I even have one."

"Everyone must have one. I'll just give you one then." She crossed her arms over her chest and surveyed him from head to toe. His body heated under her perusal. She tapped her finger on her chin in thought. "Banks."

"What did you say?"

"Banks. Brody Banks. I found you in the water and we landed on the banks together. So that's what I'll call you."

"All right, Gwen."

"It's Gwendolen Fisher." She made a face. "I don't like to be called Fisher, though."

"Why not? You're the daughter of a fisherman. That's your name."

"Still, I wish it could be something else."

"Then how about Banks as well?"

Gwen froze when she heard Brody's suggestion. His intense eyes drank her in and her heart skipped a beat. Why would he say a thing like that? That is, unless he was purposely trying to make it sound as if they were married. Surely, that's not what he meant. Feeling insecure and, at the same time, intensely attracted to him, her tongue felt too big for her mouth. She couldn't bring herself to answer.

While the thought of it intrigued her for some reason, she needed to remind herself he was a pirate! Her father would most likely kill Brody the next time he saw the man since he hated pirates. And if she decided to marry one without confronting him first, he might kill her as well.

"We'd better hurry if we're going to make it to the tavern before darkness sets in." She turned on her heel and started to climb the rocks. When she glanced back, she noticed his eyes on her backside. That made her smile. Something did happen in the cave whether he wanted to admit it or not. So, mayhap the lovers' legend wasn't such nonsense after all.

They made it to the Three Gulls quickly. When

Gwen realized Brody limped even more than before, she put her arm around him, and they entered through the front door of the establishment.

"That'll be a halfpence each," said the guard at the door. He held a piece of wood in his hand. His job was to collect the entrance fee that would help pay for any damages should a fight occur. The man would test the coins to see if they were real, by bouncing them on the wood.

"I'm sorry, I don't have any money," said Gwen, looking at Brody.

"Don't look at me. It's not like my crew loaded me down with coins before they made me walk the plank," Brody mumbled.

"Walk the plank?" The guard lowered the board to his side. His eyes scanned the room. He leaned over and whispered in a rough voice. "Pirates are free. Go on in."

"What makes you think he's a pirate?" asked Gwen.

"Don't ask questions." Brody took her by the elbow and escorted her into the tavern. "Now, let's just hope that food and ale and a room for the night are free for pirates as well."

Gwen gripped on to Brody's arm, frightened by what she saw. Drunken, dirty, rugged men lifted tankards and bottles to their mouths, guzzling down the liquid and belching loudly. A few of them had whores on their laps. The place smelled like wood smoke from the fire and there was no mistaking the strong scent of whisky. The rushes under their feet were soiled and reeked from urine. The smell of the place made her want to retch.

"Let's find a table." Brody pulled her over to a small table in a dark corner, plopping down on a chair, running his hand over his injured leg. The cloth was bright red with new blood.

"You're bleeding again," she said, genuinely concerned for his health. "We need to find help."

"There's no one here that'll be interested in helping me."

"I'll go ask."

His hand clamped around her wrist. "Take a seat, sweetheart. If you go out into that sea of sharks, you're nothing but fresh bait."

She looked over to see all the men staring at her. Pushing her long hair behind her shoulder, she wished now she had it tucked into a cap so they'd think she was a boy. "I suppose you're right." She sank into a chair opposite him. The place was noisy and dark. She didn't like it. It reminded her of the time she'd seen her father and brothers in here. That night her father discovered her and threatened to punish her if she ever told her mother.

Brody grabbed two tankards of ale from a serving wench's tray, handing one to Gwen.

"You need to pay for that," said the woman, putting one hand on her hip.

"Keep track. We'll pay later. And bring us some food." Brody took a swig of ale.

"We don't take credit from strangers," spat the woman.

"Brody's not a stranger. He grew up in Cornwall," Gwen told her.

"Brody?" A man overheard them and walked toward them from across the room.

"Aye, that's my name." Brody took another swig of ale, looking over the rim of his cup at the man. Then he slowly put the vessel down on the table. "Who are you?"

"Brody, is that you?" asked the man with a smile. "Don't you recognize your old friend, Edwin? I wondered what happened to you all those years ago."

Gwen watched Brody wince in pain, bite his lip and then lean his head back against the wall. The color drained from his face and his eyes closed. He either passed out – or he was dead.

Chapter 4

Brody's eyes opened and he thought he'd been dreaming. Could the man standing in front of him really be his old friend, Edwin?

"Edwin," he whispered, sitting up straight, not at all sure he hadn't passed out for a moment. Feeling lightheaded and tired, all he wanted to do was eat and sleep. "Is it really you?"

"God's eyes, I thought the pirates had killed you." Edwin pulled up a stool and sat with them at the table.

"He's hurt and starving," said Gwen.

"Abigail, hurry and bring us some food." Edwin motioned to the same serving girl who had scowled at them when Brody took the ale. "More ale, too."

"But they have no money," complained the girl, raising a brow. "I hope this isn't another one of those pirates you let in here for free."

"Just bring it," commanded Edwin. His eyes

dropped to Brody's leg. "Have Anthony prepare a room for my friend. Set up a bath and get some healing herbs and thread. He's wounded."

The girl left, talking to herself.

"Are you the friend Brody told me about that dared him to carve his name on the wall of the cave?" asked Gwen.

"Aye," Edwin answered with a chuckle. "That I am. And who are you?"

"I'm Gwen. Gwen . . . Banks," she said, looking over at Brody.

Brody groaned inwardly. Why had he ever suggested she take the same surname she'd given him? It had slipped from his tongue so easily, but now he wished he could take back the suggestion.

"She's with you?" Edwin raised a brow at Brody.

"She's the daughter of a fisherman named Cato Fisher." Brody drained the tankard and thunked it down on the table.

"Did you say, Cato?" Edwin's face darkened.

"Have you seen my father?" asked Gwen anxiously. "We were thrown off the ship in a storm after lightning hit the mast."

"Nay. I haven't seen him in a while now," said Edwin. "Not since his sons left him to pirate the seas on their own."

"What?" Gwen blinked twice. "My brothers, Aaron, Tristan, and Mardon are not pirates. They wanted more from life than to be fishermen and that's why they left.

They all have respectable jobs working overseas."

Edwin chuckled. "Who told you that?"

"My father," she snapped.

"I see Captain Cato has managed to keep the truth from his only daughter all these years."

"My father is a captain of a fishing ship. He's a fisherman."

"Listen, Gwen. I think I ought to know better than anyone whose fault it is that pirates come in here all the time demanding free food and drink or they'll kill us," Edwin told her. "Your father and brothers were the ones who started it years ago. If I ever see Cato again, I'll give him a piece of my mind."

"Here's some pottage and fresh brown bread." The serving wench slapped it down on the table. "I'll be back with more ale. And Anthony says the room is ready. The water is still being heated for the tub, but they can go up whenever they want. Your wife is getting a needle and thread for your friend as well."

"Thank you, Abigail." Edwin reached into his pocket and flipped her a coin. She smiled, stuck it in her cleavage and left the table.

Brody was so hungry that he dug into the food. Ripping off a hunk of bread, he dipped it in the bowl of pottage that would be shared by everyone at the table. Then he shoveled it into his mouth. "You're married?" he asked, not looking up but continuing to eat.

"I am. How about you? Is this your wife?" asked Edwin.

Brody glanced up to see Gwen looking like she was about to cry. "Here, Gwen. Have some food." He pushed the bowl over to her. He'd been so hungry that he hadn't even thought that she might want some.

"I'm not hungry." She pushed it back. "And my father is not a pirate."

Edwin and Brody's eyes interlocked. Brody shook his head slightly, warning his friend not to continue.

"If you're not hungry, why don't you wait for me in the room?" suggested Brody. "You take the first bath. It'll warm your bones."

"I'll have my wife wash and dry your clothes by the fire," said Edwin.

"Aye." She stood as if in a daze.

"Marta, come here." Edwin flagged down his wife who came to join them. "This is my childhood friend, Brody, and this is Gwen."

"I'm happy to meet you," said the woman. She was a short woman with a round face and a big smile. Her stomach looked very large. Brody was sure she was pregnant.

"We're having our first baby soon," she told them, rubbing her belly.

"I'm happy for you," said Brody. "Would you mind taking Gwen upstairs? I'll be there soon."

"Of course." The woman took Gwen by the arm and directed her toward the stairs. "I'll tend to your wound when you're ready," she called over her shoulder.

Once the women left, Brody continued eating.

Abigail plunked two tankards of ale on the table and left. He grabbed one and chugged down the liquid.

"Slow down," laughed Edwin. "You are eating and drinking as if you haven't had food in a sennight."

"I haven't." Brody finished off the pottage and pushed back in his chair and sighed.

"Well, are you going to tell me what happened?" asked Edwin.

"I was taken by pirates. You know that."

"Aye. I returned to the cave with men from the village to rescue you, but the ship was already gone. I'm sorry, Brody. I've thought of you every day since it happened. It should have been me they abducted, but you gave yourself up to them instead. How can I ever repay you?"

"I did it because you were a good friend, Edwin. I had nothing to lose, but you had everything. You had a family and siblings and a business that would be yours someday."

"The inn is mine now, Brody. My father died. My brother, Anthony, helps me to run it. And I'm happily married with a child on the way. I owe everything to you. Just tell me what I can do to help you and I'll do it."

"Take back that comment you made about Gwen's father and brothers being pirates," he mumbled.

"I wish I could." He looked over his shoulder at the women climbing the stairs. "Unfortunately, it's true. We were young and didn't realize it, but my father ended up telling me everything. Cato was a drunk and not very good as a fisherman either. His wife threatened to leave him if he couldn't support the family. He started to pirate just to get what they needed to survive. When his sons got older, they joined him. But they kept the truth from Cato's wife and daughter. One night, his wife found out. They fought and he pushed her. She hit her head and died. I am sure he never told Gwen the truth of how her mother passed away."

"No, I don't think she knows. What happened to Gwen's brothers?"

"After their mother died, they blamed their father for everything. They decided to leave. They took his ship and haven't returned since. Cato managed to secure another ship, but it's nothing compared to the Falcon."

"Then Gwen's brothers are still pirates?"

"They are, as far as I know."

"The Falcon," Brody said in thought. "God's toes, I know that ship. We had a run in with it years ago. One-Eyed Ron made a deal with the captain. They had rights to the channel and we claimed the territory on the west coast."

"So that's why they've never returned."

"And that's why Gwen's old man hates pirates."

"It is a part of him that's ruined his life," said Edwin. "It has ruined yours, too, Brody. I'm sorry."

"It didn't ruin my life. While I rejected One-Eyed Ron and his crew at first, I ended up meeting Rowen.

He was a boy when they abducted him as well. He's a wonderful man and my best friend now."

"Really. Then why did he make you walk the plank?" Edwin raised his brows.

"Nay, it wasn't him. Rowen is one of the bastard triplets of King Edward. He once raided the king under the guise of being the Demon Thief. Now he pays his father fealty instead."

"Aye, I've heard the story. Word travels fast."

"He gave me the Sea Mirage, but now my crew has become mutinous. I don't believe he even knows about it. I need to get back to Whitehaven to talk to him."

"I'll lend you a horse and cart. As soon as your leg is better, you can go. But what about the girl?"

Brody's eyes traveled to the stairs that led to the rooms overhead. His heart went out to Gwen. She didn't deserve to be lied to. He was going to have to tell her the whole truth about her father and brothers. How could he let her go back to a man like that? All Brody wanted was to protect her.

"I can't leave her here. We don't even know if her father is alive. The ship got damaged badly in the storm. Even if he did survive, I don't think she'd want to go back to him once she hears he's the one responsible for the disappearance of her brothers and the death of her mother."

"Then what are you going to do?" asked Edwin.

Brody pushed up from the table, knowing what he would do. It was the answer to all Gwen's problems.

"I'm going to protect her," he said. "Edwin, I know this sounds odd, but remember that wall in the cave that I carved my name into all those years ago?"

"Of course." Edwin stood as well. "How could I ever forget?"

"Have you ever heard of a crazy legend that if two people touch it at the same time, they'll fall in love?"

Edwin laughed. "My wife believes that, but I think it's only a wretched lie made up by a love-struck woman."

"I thought so at first, too. But now I'm not so certain." Brody could think of naught else but Gwen. How could he go through life never seeing her again? He wanted to be there for her and to protect her from souses like her father. She needed him in her life, even if she deserved someone so much better.

"You aren't starting to believe that alewives' gossip, are you?"

"I touched the wall at the same time as Gwen." Brody's eyes traveled to the stairs. He needed to get back to her side.

"And you're saying you two are in love now?"

"Nay, I'm not saying that at all. That would be ridiculous. But I do feel something for her. We kissed and now I can't think of anything but being with her."

"It's lust, Brody. Mayhap I can lend you one of the whores for the night." Edwin raised his hand in the air and started to call one over.

"Nay, it's not lust." Brody reached out and lowered

his friend's hand. "It's more than that. I can't explain it. It's like I've known her my entire life although I've just met her. When I'm with her, it feels right. I can't believe I'm saying this, but I can see spending the rest of my life with her, Edwin."

"Brody, this doesn't sound like you. What are you going to do?"

"I'm going to do the only thing that will take her away from her father and all the hurt she's endured - or is going to have to face when she knows the entire truth about her family."

"What does that mean, you fool?"

"It means I'm going to ask her to marry me."

Chapter 5

Gwen sank into the tub of hot water, trying to stop crying. Had she been so gullible her entire life that she didn't know her father had once been a pirate? She wouldn't believe it if she hadn't seen him and her brothers in the tavern years ago with their booty. It all made sense now. She'd never mentioned it to her father, but she did tell her mother what she'd seen that night. It was right afterward that her mother slipped on the floor and died.

With her eyes closed and her head partially under the water, she didn't even hear Brody enter the room. But when she opened her eyes, there he was, standing at the other end of the tub, staring down at her. She sank lower, crossing her arms over her chest.

"I didn't hear you come into the room. Why didn't you make your presence known?"

"You looked so peaceful and comfortable. I didn't

want to disturb you."

"I'll get out so you can use the bath."

"Don't bother." He pulled off his headscarf and then his torn tunic. His fingers reached for his belt.

"Why not?" she asked, sure he meant they could use the tub together. Part of her was excited by that idea. Still, she was terrified at the same time.

"I don't think it's a good idea to soak my wound in the soapy water."

"Oh." She sat up slightly and the water splashed over the rim. "I'll get out then. Will you please turn around?"

"Of course." He turned around, bending over to kick off his boots. She hurriedly exited the tub and wrapped herself in a drying cloth big enough to cover her body. "Marta has taken my clothes to clean them. She left me one of her gowns to wear in the meantime. She said it won't fit her right now since she's pregnant. She left you a pair of her husband's breeches and a tunic."

She removed the towel and reached for the gown. He turned around just then.

"Oh!" She clutched the tunic to her chest. Their eyes met. The fire illuminated the outline of his body. Most rooms at an inn didn't have a hearth, but this room was the one usually used by Edwin and his wife since they were the proprietors.

"You – you're beautiful," he said, his eyes still fastened to her.

"You are very handsome yourself."

"I don't know why you hide under those clothes of a boy. You are a woman and should be proud of it."

"Here." Holding the towel in front of her with one hand, she gave him Edwin's clothes with the other. "I'll just be a minute."

Their hands brushed against each other when he took the clothes. It was enough to send a flittering tingle up her arm. He jerked backward at the same time.

"You felt it, too, didn't you?"

"I did," he admitted. "I also felt something between us in the cave."

"Why did you lie then?" Her hands trembled.

"I don't know. I guess I didn't want to admit that something so beautiful could come from a place that holds dark memories of my past."

"You mean the cave. When the pirates took you, right?"

"Aye." He turned around, allowing her the privacy to dress. When she donned the gown and faced him again, he was naked, putting on the breeches.

A gasp caught in her throat when she saw his well-toned body. Brody wasn't the tallest man she'd ever met, but he had muscles just as large as any sailor. He fastened the tie around his waist, not bothering with the tunic. Then he sat down on the edge of the bed, rolling up one leg of the breeches, inspecting his unwrapped wound.

"Oh, how thoughtless of me. Please, let me help

you." She ran over to him, picking up a cloth from the bed along the way. "Let me see that."

Brody felt Gwen's body heat next to him and then the gentle touch of her slim fingers on his leg. He'd discovered downstairs his wound didn't need to be stitched. It was just a flesh wound and probably hurt so bad since it was on the joint.

"I'll clean it properly this time." She used a rag and water from the tub, rinsing the soap off the wound with clean water from a ceramic ewer. "It doesn't look as bad as I thought." She sat down next to him and wrapped the cloth around his wound.

Brody could smell rose water in her wet hair. It was intoxicating. He couldn't help himself. He leaned over and kissed her on the head. She stopped and turned her face upward.

"What was that for?"

"I was . . . thanking you for caring for me. It's been a long time since anyone has done that."

Her lips turned up in a smile. Then she boldly reached out and kissed him on the mouth. Her essence filled his senses, making his heart swell. It felt right to be with Gwen. He wasn't sure if it was because of the silly legend or just fate, but he honestly cared for her.

"What was that for?" he asked in return.

"You saved my life when I fell from the ship in the storm," she answered.

"I see." He lifted her chin gently and kissed her

again. This time the kiss lingered. He wasn't in a hurry to pull away. "That's for saving my life when you plucked me from the sea to begin with."

Her eyes closed slightly and she relaxed, her body leaning up against his chest. Her lips glistened and her cheeks were rosy. The flames in the hearth flickered, causing shadows to dance over her face. To him, she looked like an angel. He brushed back a curl of her wet hair.

"I suppose this could go on all night," she commented.

"I'd like it to, Gwen. I've never met anyone like you before. But there is something we need to discuss."

Her body immediately went rigid. "I don't want to talk about my father and brothers being pirates because it's not true."

"Edwin told me more. It is true and I think you know it."

Tears fell from her eyes. He brushed them away with his thumb. Finally, she sighed and nodded. "Aye. I think I knew the truth for a long time now but didn't want to admit it. I just wanted my family to be the way it used to be so long ago when I was a child. We were happy then. We didn't have much, but neither did it matter. We had each other."

"Edwin said your father took to pirating to support your family. Your mother didn't know about it. When she found out, they argued. Cato pushed her and she fell – and died."

"Nay!" Her big, blue-green orbs looked up in horror as she shook her head.

"Yes, Gwen. It was an accident, I'm sure. But your father is responsible for the death of your mother."

"He's not," she said, shaking her head vigorously. The tears flowed faster now.

"You're going to have to stop denying the truth, no matter how hard it may be to accept it."

"My father didn't kill her."

"You don't know that."

"I do. Because, I killed her, Brody."

"What are you saying?"

"I wasn't supposed to tell my mother I saw them in the tavern that night. But I was only ten years old. Of course, I told her. So, you see, I'm the reason they argued. I'm responsible for my mother's death."

"Shhh," he told her, cradling her head against his chest and rocking her gently. "It was an accident and you are not to blame. She would have found out sooner or later and they still would have argued."

"Oh, Brody, I hope I'm not the reason my brothers left as well."

"Edwin told me that after your mother's death, your father took to the bottle. They'd had enough of his antics. Your brothers stole his ship and left."

"Yes, they left a few years after my mother died. Why would they leave me behind?"

"I don't have the answers, Gwen, but a pirate ship is no place for a young woman. They might have thought leaving you behind was safer."

"Nay, I won't believe they are really pirates! It can't be true."

"It is, Gwen. The Sea Mirage confronted their ship, the Falcon, a few years back. We made a deal. They were sent to raid up and down the channel while we controlled the west coast."

"You saw my brothers? So they really are pirates?"

"I don't know them personally but I'm sure they were on the ship. I vaguely remember hearing their names."

"I need to know for sure." She dabbed at her tears with the sleeve of her gown.

"I suppose we'll never really know."

"Yes, we will." She sat up straighter and lifted her chin. "When my father returns, I am going to confront him and ask him all about this."

"*If* he returns." Brody felt like a scoundrel, secretly wishing the man had died at sea, but it would be the best for Gwen. Then she wouldn't have to feel the hurt of this whole situation. Plus, it would be better for him, because he had a feeling her father was not going to sit still once he found out that Brody planned on marrying his daughter.

Chapter 6

Brody slept all night with Gwen cuddled up against his chest. After he had confronted her with the truth about her family last night, he thought he needed to give her time to accept it all. But he still planned on asking her to marry him, and he wanted to do it before her father showed up. Marrying her felt like the right thing to do.

She awoke a few minutes after him. Stretching and yawning, she reminded him of a cute little kitten waking from a nap.

"Sleep well?" he asked, running his hand up and down her back.

"Aye. And you?" She wiped the sleep out of her eyes with the back of her hand.

"Sure." After collapsing from sheer exhaustion, he had slept most of the night. But when he awoke in the dark with Gwen pressed up against his body, there was no more sleeping. He wanted her badly, however, there was no way he'd take her until they were married. She deserved better than a romp in bed with a pirate before they'd taken their vows. She might act and dress like a lad but all he wanted to do was treat her like a lady.

"Brody?" Her long lashes blinked. "Is something troubling you?"

"Nay. Not really."

"Oh, my." She sat up on the bed. "I was so distraught about my problems, I've forgotten about yours. Is your leg hurting?"

"Just a little."

"Let me take a look." He took her hand in his to stop her.

"There is something on my mind after all."

"It's about your childhood and being taken by pirates, isn't it? Tell me about it. Please."

"I already told you. I was an orphan, so I fought off the pirates to make them release Edwin. They took me instead."

She looked at him in awe. "That was such a noble thing to do for a friend."

"I had less to lose than Edwin. And I know it sounds strange, but the pirates ended up replacing the family I lost."

"That's preposterous. How can you say that? Were these the same pirates that made you walk the plank and tried to drown you at sea?"

"No! Yes. How do you know about that?"

"You made the comment when we arrived about walking the plank. You also said you were a captain, so I just assumed that's what happened."

"Well, that's only partially right. Two pirates managed to escape the dungeon when the former captain – Rowen – put them there. Old Man Muck and Lucky Dog returned and were responsible for what happened to me."

She laughed. "Are those really their names?"

"They are to us. That's all anyone has ever called them. Muck and Lucky came back and convinced the crew that Rowen wanted me dumped at sea."

"Did he?"

"Nay, I'm sure he didn't. Rowen is a lot like me and was also stolen by pirates at a young age. We were like brothers growing up."

"He didn't have siblings, either?"

"On the contrary, he is a triplet. And they happen to be King Edward's bastards."

"That's right," she said, nodding her head. "I've heard of them. They were once referred to as the Demon Thief."

"I need to find Rowen and talk to him. I'm sure he never gave such an order."

"You need to find Muck and Lucky."

"Aye. And when I do, I'll kill them."

She jerked backward in surprise. "Spoken like a true pirate."

That hurt Brody, and she obviously could see it by the expression on his face.

"I'm sorry, I didn't mean that." Her hand covered his. "What was it you wanted to talk to me about?"

Brody suddenly started having doubt. Mayhap a marriage between them wasn't the answer. Although he didn't start out as a pirate, it was how he ended up. Gwen already had a family of pirates and didn't need one more in her life. Perhaps he should just let her go.

"I thought we could go for a walk along the shore," he told her.

"I would like that," she answered with a smile, looking deeply into his eyes. He almost reached out and kissed her again but stopped with her next words. "Then we can watch for my father.

An hour later, Gwen walked hand in hand along the beach with Brody, feeling more like a girl than she had in a very long time. Her hair was braided, hanging down her back and not covered with a hat. Instead of a tunic and breeches like she usually wore, she had donned one of Marta's gowns. It was plain, and far from fancy, but it was a dress meant for a woman.

"You look . . . so different," she said to Brody, almost laughing at seeing him in Edwin's clothes. Edwin was shorter than Brody, so his sleeves and the legs of the breeches were short. He'd tied his long hair back and covered his head with a hat instead of the red scarf he usually wore. As he walked with a limp, she could tell he was trying to hold back the pain.

"Is it the clothes you're talking about or the fact I'm limping around like a one-legged pirate?"

She giggled, and that made him smile too. "How about if we sit down so you can rest your leg?"

They made their way to some large rocks jutting out of the water and sat down. Brody took off his shoes and soaked his feet in the sea.

"That looks like fun. I'll do it too." She followed suit, kicking her legs and splashing water on both of them.

"Two can play that game," he told her, kicking his legs as well, managing to get both of them wet.

She held up her hands to block the water from her face, squinting and laughing. "No more," she said. "I've had enough water lately to last me a lifetime."

"You?" he asked with a chuckle. "And what about me? If I am around water much longer, I swear I'll turn into a fish."

"You do that and I'll turn into a mermaid and lure you off your ship." She kissed him, and his hands went around her waist. With the sea air in her hair and the waves lapping at her feet, she felt happy and free.

"There you go talking about legends again, Gwen."

"Oh, I forgot. You don't believe in them. Sorry."

"Well . . . mayhap not all of them."

"What do you mean?"

"That legend of the lovers' cave might have some truth to it after all."

"You believe it?" She sat up straight and her eyes opened wide.

"I can't say I believe anything actually happened there except for the obvious – me being kidnapped."

"Then why did you mention it?"

"I mentioned it, because ever since I kissed you in the cave, I can't seem to stop doing it."

"It is nice, isn't it?" She bit her bottom lip and peeked up at him through her lashes.

"More than nice, Gwen. It feels right to me. I can't explain it, but it is as if I've always known you. I am comfortable around you."

"I feel that way, too."

"I think . . . I'm starting to have feelings for you."

"You are?" Her breath hitched and her heart picked up a beat. "I also have feelings for you."

"You are a beautiful young woman who deserves so much more." His fingers trailed over her cheek.

"What does that mean? More than what?"

"Gwen, I wanted to ask you – I mean, I was thinking mayhap . . . no, it's probably not a good idea." He shook his head. "We should just forget about it."

"Forget about what?" she almost shouted. "You haven't told me a thing. Spit it out, Brody. What is it you are trying to say?" She kept at it, until Brody finally answered.

"Marry me!" he shouted.

She stopped, too shocked to know how to respond to that. Her silence seemed to make him more apprehensive than before.

"Let's put our shoes on and walk back to the inn for a bit to eat." He picked up his shoes, not looking at her at all.

"Yes," she answered softly, just staring at him and not able to move. Was this really happening?

"Yes?" He looked up, still putting on his shoes. "Yes to walking or eating?"

"To marrying you."

"Oh." He dropped a shoe, and his eyes interlocked with hers. "Are you sure? I mean – mayhap it isn't a good idea after all. What will your father say? And do you really want to marry a pirate?"

She was tired of all his questions. As her heart swelled with emotion, she got that feeling in her chest again. Just like he said, they were meant to be together. She threw her arms around his neck and kissed him over and over. His arms closed around her and they both fell back on the rock.

"Easy there," he told her. "We don't want to be worn out before the wedding night."

"Oh, Brody, I'm very excited. I know this is all so fast, but just like you said, I feel as if we've known each other forever. Yes, I want to be your wife."

"Aye, but I don't think your father will feel the same way."

"My father." She sat up, looking out to the sea. "I don't even know if he's alive or if he perished in the storm."

Brody took her hands in his and stared deeply into her eyes. "Gwen, your father might never return."

"Don't say that. I'm sure he will. He might be stranded at sea. I wish we could look for him."

"The mast was broken and the ship damaged." He shook his head. "I don't want you to get your hopes up. It was a bad storm."

"My father is an experienced sailor. I'm sure he survived."

"I hope you're right, Gwen. For your sake, I hope you're right."

Chapter 7

It had been three days, and still, there was no sign of Cato or his ship. Brody's leg was feeling much better, and he walked the beach with Gwen several times, looking for wreckage. They found pieces of a mast, planks, and cargo as well. They couldn't be certain it was from her father's ship, but Gwen seemed to think so.

"I had Edwin send a few of his workers up the coast to some of the neighboring ports to ask if anyone has seen your father," said Brody. "They returned this morning."

"What did they say?" she asked anxiously. "Has anyone seen him or his crew?"

"Nay. There has been some more wreckage that washed to shore, but no bodies."

"That's good," she said, nodding, looking at the

ground. "That means there is still a chance he's alive."

"Gwen, sweetheart," he said, taking her hands in his. "I can't stand to see you put yourself through this. Face the fact that your father is never coming back."

"Hold me, Brody," she begged, wrapping her arms around him. Together they stood and stared out to sea. "Why does it feel so frightening being all alone?"

"You're not alone, sweetheart. You've got me now."

"I always thought I was strong and didn't need anyone," she confessed. "But after what's happened lately, I have changed my mind. I miss my family. Family is everything, yet why is it we don't realize it until it's all been taken away?"

"Someday soon, we'll make our own family," he told her. "And our children will not be orphans like the two of us."

She looked up with sad eyes, longing showing in her gaze.

"When will that be, Brody?"

"When we marry, we'll have plenty of children," he told her.

"I don't want to wait."

He chuckled. "It's short notice to find a priest."

"Then we'll start making children before we take our vows."

"Gwen," he said, rubbing a hand over her back. "What are you saying?"

"I'm saying I don't ever want to be alone again. I

don't like the feeling. I wanted to wait until my father returned before we married, but now I see that might never happen. Make love to me, Brody. Let's seal our deal now, and not wait a moment longer."

"You don't mean that." He smoothed down her hair with his hand. The wind had picked up, and it was becoming chilly.

"I do. Take me back to the inn and let's start raising a family right away."

"I'm not sure your father will like the idea."

"My father is never coming back, and you know it. The sea has claimed him. I'm alone now. I'll never find my brothers again, and even if I did – they are pirates."

Brody didn't want to take the time to ask her what she meant by that. Did she forget he was a pirate too? Mayhap now wasn't the time to remind her of that.

It didn't take long to get back to their room. Gwen didn't hesitate to remove her clothes and climb under the covers, waiting for him.

"Brody? Why aren't you joining me in bed?" she asked.

He dragged a weary hand through his long hair. "I don't want you to regret this in the morning. I have a feeling I am your first lover, and that I will be taking from you something that can never be returned."

The smile on her face disappeared. She reached out and picked at invisible lint atop the blanket. "Would you change your mind about marrying me if I wasn't a virgin?"

"Gwen, what are you saying?" He walked over and sat down on the edge of the bed.

"My father was very protective of me. Especially after my mother died and my brothers left us."

"As he should be. If I have daughters someday, I will be protective of them as well."

"Nay, you don't understand." A look of despair washed over her face. He could see something was troubling her.

"Gwen, is something wrong?" He reached out and took her hands in his. "Tell me about it, please."

"Nay," she said, shaking her head. A lone tear trailed down her cheek. He bent over and kissed it away. The salty taste lingered on his tongue. "You won't want me if you know the truth of what I did."

"How can you say that? After all, you know my past has been very tarnished, and yet you still want to marry me."

"That's different. You had no choice about your past. You were stolen by pirates and did what you had to, just to survive."

"We all have choices in life, Gwen. Even in the direst of situations. I had no family and chose to accept the pirates because, like you, I didn't want to be alone."

"I only did it to spite my father," she said through her tears. "I didn't know what would happen or I would never have gone down that path."

"I don't know what you're talking about unless you tell me. But I promise you, whatever you did in the past won't matter to me. I'll still want you for my wife, just the same."

"Really?" she asked him, looking up with a renewed hope in her eyes.

"I promise," he said, sealing his vow with a kiss.

She took a deep breath and released it, and then nodded slowly. "All right. You deserve the truth, so I'll tell you. It wasn't long after my brothers left us. I was feeling sad. I blamed their leaving on my father since I heard them arguing that night. My father threatened me never to try to leave him. He said he was going to protect me and no one would lay a hand on me for as long as I lived."

"What's wrong with that?" asked Brody. "I would think you'd be happy that your father cared so much for you."

"Nay. You don't understand. He said he never wanted me to leave him. He didn't want me ever to marry or even be with a man."

"Oh. I see." Brody removed his clothes and climbed under the covers with Gwen, pulling her close in his arms. With her bare skin pressed up against his, it felt alluring. "So what did you do?"

"I was much too young, but I decided I was going to couple with a man, just because my father didn't want me to. I was bold and cocky . . . and naïve and stupid."

"How so?"

"We were on the ship – on a fishing trip. I purposely went down in the hold with the son of one of my father's friends. He was about my age. I seduced him and lured him into coupling with me right there in the hold. My father caught us."

"Oh. That can't have been good."

"I wanted my father to know that I'd coupled and that he couldn't control me anymore." Her tears fell faster. "I never thought he'd kill the boy."

"He did?" Brody asked in surprise.

"He strangled him with his bare hands. I was so frightened that I did nothing to help. I just stood there and watched. And when the boy's father came down to the hold next, a fight broke out between my father and his best friend."

"Can you blame him? Your father killed his son."

"My father has a bad temper. He never meant to kill the boy, but his anger got the best of him. Because of me. It was my fault the boy died." She cried harder, hiding her head against his chest. He comforted her and held her tight against him.

"You were young and didn't know how your father would react," said Brody. "The boy's death wasn't your fault."

"My father killed his best friend that day, too. But that was an act of self-defense. Then he dumped both bodies overboard and swore the crew to secrecy of what really happened. He said if anyone leaked a word of the truth, he'd kill them too."

"So, your father's friend – did he have a wife and other children?"

"Nay," she said, sniffing. "That was the only good that came from the situation. There was no one waiting for them back home that would miss them. That's the day my father started drinking whisky instead of ale. His drinking got more and more out of control, and it is all my fault."

"Shhh, it's no one's fault," he said, holding her close and looking over the top of her head. Now, he wondered what would happen if Cato returned and found out they made love. He didn't fancy being at the end of a drunken, mad man's blade.

"That was a horrible thing he did, and I should have known right then and there he was a pirate," she mumbled into his chest.

"Not all pirates are like that," he told her.

"Nay, you're wrong," she said. "And I'm sure my brothers are like that now as well."

"Gwen, mayhap we should wait on making love," he told her, hearing malice dripping from her words. If she hated pirates that much, why had she agreed to marry him? And would she change her mind about him several years down the road?

"I'm sorry, Brody. I should never have lured you to my bed. In a way, I suppose I'm a pirate too - doing whatever it takes to get what I want."

"I know a lot of people like that, Gwen. It's not just pirates that act that way. Now, I suggest we both get some shut-eye. We'll still hold each other tonight, and in the morning we can think about things with a clear head." As soon as he said it, he knew how addlepated he was acting. God's eyes, how was he going to sleep with a beautiful, naked woman in his arms and not take her before the morning?

Chapter 8

A knock at the door the next morning had them both bolting from the bed. Gwen wrapped the sheet around her, and got there first. She was about to open it, when Brody's hand shot forward, holding the door closed. He was in his braies.

"You need always to be certain first that there isn't anyone on the other side of the door that will hurt you."

"You are starting to sound like my father."

"Brody, open up, it's Edwin," came the muffled voice through the thick wood.

Brody swung the door open. "What is it that can't wait until we're out of bed?"

Edwin looked at him and Gwen and smiled. "I see."

"It's not what you think," he said, feeling embarrassed for Gwen. "Now, what do you want?"

"It's Gwen's father."

"Did you find him?" she asked, excitedly, almost

dropping the sheet. "Is he alive? How about the ship and crew?"

"The ship just sailed into port, but it's busted up badly," announced Edwin. "The crew was lost at sea, but the old man managed to somehow bring the ship in by himself."

"My father!" shouted Gwen. "I've got to see him."

"We'll be right down," Brody told Edwin and closed the door.

"I'm so glad he's still alive." Gwen hurriedly dressed and pushed her feet into her shoes. Then she headed over to a trunk with a boar's bristle brush sitting atop it. "I hope Marta won't mind if I borrow her brush, but I want to look my best for Father. He's never seen me in a gown before."

"Never?" Brody finished dressing and limped over to join her.

"Nay. My family didn't have a lot of money. That is a good part of the reason I grew up wearing my brothers' old clothes. I must say, I like the way I look in a gown."

"So do I. Here, let me." He gently took the brush from her, running it over her hair, using his other hand to smooth it down. "I thought you'd be angry with your father after the story you told me last night."

"That happened a long time ago, Brody. And it was my fault it ever happened at all. I can't put all the blame on him. It was my decision that put everyone in that horrible position."

"I suppose you're right. He stopped and ran his hand over the boar bristles. "But what about the part that he is a pirate?"

"Was a pirate. He's not one anymore."

"Once a pirate always a pirate," he muttered, wondering if he would be able to change.

"I know I should be angry, but he's the only family I have. Besides, when I tell him I'm the one responsible for my mother's death, it'll be a weight off his shoulders. Mayhap he'll stop drinking."

"Gwen, I don't want you to get your hopes up," he told her, brushing out her hair once again. "Sometimes, it's hard for people to change and they never give up their old ways."

"Are you going to give up being a pirate?" she asked, surprising him by her question. His hands stilled on her hair.

"I'd like to," he said. "Although, I would like to get my ship back as well. The sea is such a big part of my life. I don't know how I'd ever live on land again."

"Brody, forget about killing Muck and Lucky. Talk to Rowen and find your ship, but no more killing. Please."

He put the brush down on a trunk and turned her to face him. "That's part of what I wanted to talk to you about last night. I feel as if I'm ready for a change in life."

"Will you give up the sea?"

"Nay." He shook his head. "The sea is in my heart. I

don't ever want to stop sailing."

"Then be a fisherman like my father."

"A fisherman?" He laughed. "That would be so boring after the exciting life I've lived."

"Then I guess you don't want to give up being a pirate after all." She stepped around him and rushed to the door.

"Wait, Gwen. I'm not done talking."

"My father might be hurt. I have to go to him. He needs me."

Gwen rushed from the room, not waiting for Brody to answer. Why had she thought he'd agree to change since they planned on getting married? Mayhap it was because she wanted it so desperately. She had already envisioned a small cottage by the sea filled with their children.

Sleeping in his arms last night had made it feel as if they were already married, even though they hadn't coupled. She didn't want him to walk away from her now. But he sounded as if he would never give up being a pirate. She had secretly hoped he would choose her over the sea, but now she realized that he'd always be a pirate in his heart.

By the time she got down the stairs, the door to the inn had opened. Several men carried her father into the building, laying him atop one of the long tables.

"Father!" She ran to her father, pushing her way through the crowd.

"Gwen, is that you? Thank God you're alive. I thought you drowned at sea." His head had a deep gash on it, and his clothes were tattered and wet. His skin looked like worn leather, and his teeth were broken with his lip split. He looked so frail.

"Don't bring that bloody pirate in here," spat Edwin, coming to the front of the crowd. "Get him out of here, now!"

"Nay!" Gwen covered her father's body with hers, stretching out her arms. "Leave him here. He's wounded."

"Gwen, Daughter." Her father could barely keep his eyes open as he struggled to take her hands in his. "It doesn't matter because I'm near death."

"Don't say that! You'll be fine." The tears dripped down her cheeks.

"The only thing that kept me alive was my will to find you and tell you I love you."

Gwen's heart soared. Her father had never told her he loved her before. "I love you, too, Father." She pulled back a little to look at him, smiling, and running a hand over his face.

"What are you wearing?"

"It's a gown. Do you like the way I look?"

Tears formed in his eyes. "You look so much like your mother. I was wrong to keep you from being a woman, Gwen. I'm sorry for that, as well as all the other horrible things I've done."

"I love you, Father. Please, don't die."

"I haven't been honest with you, Gwen. I need you to know the truth before I'm gone."

"I know everything. I don't care if you were a pirate. You are no longer one." Gwen stood up proudly.

"You know?"

"I know you only did it to support your family. And you weren't the one to kill Mother, I was. I told her I saw you and my brothers in the tavern that night."

"I don't want you ever to think it was your fault." His hand lifted to touch her face, but he dropped it again since he was so weak. His voice became softer, and he could barely keep his eyes open now. She could tell he was in a lot of pain. "It's my fault she's gone and also my fault that your brothers are still pirates."

"Is it true, then? They really are pirates?"

"I'm afraid so," he said with remorse in his eyes. "I only wish that I had gone after them and brought them home. There is nothing worse than a parent not going after their children."

"I'll find them, Father. I swear I will."

"I'll help her." Brody stepped forward, putting his hand on her shoulder.

"Who better to find a pirate than a pirate himself," growled Cato, ending up gagging and coughing. "You stay away from my daughter!"

"I wasn't always a pirate, and I don't plan on being one any longer," Brody said, surprising her.

"You don't?" Gwen looked at him quizzically as he continued to talk to her father.

"I'm not sure what I'll do. But I promise you that if you agree to let me marry your daughter, I will not only protect her, but I will lead the search in finding your sons."

"Brody?" Gwen looked up with tears in her eyes. "You would do that? For me?"

"I hope you still want to marry me, Gwen. I feel we belong together. I don't quite understand how it happened so quickly, but I do believe I'm falling in love with you."

"I felt that ever since we touched the cave wall."

"Not the silly legend and the wall. Really." Edwin rolled his eyes and shook his head at Brody.

"Edwin, I'm sure you love Marta and couldn't imagine a life without her," said Brody.

"Aye." His friend nodded.

"I feel as if I've been waiting a lifetime for Gwen. I don't understand why, but I feel as if we were always meant to be together."

"I agree to the wedding," came her father's faint voice.

The noise from the crowd in the tavern grew. The people moved in closer to hear more.

"Thank you, Sir," said Brody.

"I want you to have not only my daughter but also the Desperado."

"The Desperado?" asked Brody.

"That's my father's ship," explained Gwen.

"It's broken up pretty bad. However, if you fix it,

you can use it to find my sons. Please say you'll do it." Cato's grip loosened. His voice was barely above a whisper now, as his life slipped away.

"I will," answered Brody, pulling Gwen closer. "You can count on me. I will always love and take care of your daughter."

"Then I . . . can die . . . in peace." Cato's hand slipped from Gwen's as her father's life left his body. His eyes stared at the ceiling, but he didn't blink. His face was ashen, and his chest no longer moved up and down. Nor could she hear him breathing.

"Nay, don't leave me, Father." Gwen laid her body over his lifeless form, hugging him, willing him back to life.

"He's gone, sweetheart." Brody reached out and, with a gentle hand, closed her father's eyes. Then he pulled her into his arms and kissed the top of her head. "He's gone, but you're not alone because I swear I will never leave you."

Chapter 9

Brody stood staring at the Desperado the next morning after they had buried Gwen's father. The ship was in ruins from the storm. It wasn't as big as the Sea Mirage. Neither would it be as fast on the water even if he did manage to repair it. Why had he promised Cato he would help Gwen find her brothers? He didn't even have a means to do it right now.

"Thank you for everything," said Gwen walking up from the gravesite to meet him. The winds were cold since the sky had clouded over. Fall was approaching, and winter would be here soon. There was no way he'd have the repairs to the ship made before spring. "What are you thinking?" she asked, slipping her arm around his waist.

"I'm thinking how much I miss the Sea Mirage."

"Brody, did you mean what you said about giving

up being a pirate to marry me?"

He nodded, feeling the lump in his throat. His eyes remained faceted to the broken-down fishing ship. "Aye. I meant every word of it. But with this barge, we'll be lucky not to drown at sea, let alone use it to find your brothers."

"I miss Aaron, Tristan, and Mardon," she told him. "With every day that passes, their faces fade a little from my mind. I have the feeling I will never see them again."

"A lot of things can happen over time," he told her, thinking of the many years he'd spent living at sea.

"I was upset yesterday and wasn't thinking clearly when I accused you of always wanting to be a pirate. I want to tell you that I was wrong. I only said it because I was frightened that I'd lose you. Brody, I feel like I'm falling in love with you."

"You do?" He pulled her around to the front of him, embracing her in a hug.

"I do. I can't wait to be your wife."

He kissed her, and that warm feeling between them returned. A new type of excitement for life filled his being. He felt as if he'd found a lost half of himself. Aye, he was looking forward to raising a family with Gwen and being her husband.

As he kissed the top of her head, he caught sight of something from behind a cliff. A flag was wavering from atop a pole. A black flag.

"My ship!" He released Gwen and ran down to the

shore, ignoring the burning pain of the wound in his leg.

"Wait. Where are you going?" Gwen hurried after him.

"I just spotted the black flags of the Sea Mirage sailing behind the cliffs near the caves."

"You did?"

"Yes. I'm sure it's there."

They rounded the cliff and stopped. Sure enough, there was the Sea Mirage out on the water. A small transport boat with a few people was headed toward the caves.

"I see them," said Gwen, trying to catch her breath. "What are you going to do?"

"If that's Muck, I'm going to kill him." He pulled the dagger from his waistband, wishing for his sword. This was the only weapon he had right now.

"You're going to kill him with just a dagger?"

"I'll use my bare hands if I have to."

He started forward, but Gwen grabbed his arm and held him back. "Nay, wait. Please, don't kill anyone."

"He turned my crew against me. He threw me into the sea to die. Give me one reason why I shouldn't?"

"Because it's too late," came a deep voice from behind him. Brody turned around, not knowing they'd been followed. He was shocked as well as relieved to see Rowen approaching along with Edwin.

"Rowen!" he cried out, happy to see his good friend.

Gwen watched as Brody rushed over to give his friend a handshake and a slap on the back.

"I never thought I'd see you again," said Rowen.

"Rowen never stopped looking for you, ever since you were dumped in the sea," Edwin explained to Brody. "When he showed up just now asking if anyone had seen you, I knew I had to bring him to you at once."

"You must be Brody's friend that he's been telling me about," said Gwen.

"This is Gwen." Brody came back and put his arm around her and brought her forward. "We're going to get married."

"You're really doing it?" asked Edwin.

"Aye. I love her," said Brody.

"I love Brody as well," Gwen told them. "We fell in love when we touched the wall inside the cave."

"Ah, you must mean the legend of the St. Agnes cave," said Rowen.

"You believe it?" asked Brody.

"It seems to me that you two are proof enough." Rowen smiled. "Now tell me all about Gwen."

"She's Cato the pirate's daughter," blurted out Edwin.

Brody cleared his throat. "Her father just died, may he rest in peace. He was a fisherman and got caught in a nasty storm. This is Gwen. Gwen Banks."

Gwen looked up and smiled at Brody. She already

liked being treated as his wife, and they weren't even married yet.

"Rowen, you found him," came a shout from behind them. Brody turned to see Lucky running up the shore. Two more men were getting out of the transport boat.

"You!" Brody reached out and punched Lucky in the jaw, knocking him to the ground. "I'm going to kill you. Mutiny is not tolerated on the Sea Mirage."

"Brody, calm down." Rowen grabbed his fist before he could hit the man again.

"Brody, is that you?" Two more pirates rushed up to join them.

Brody looked over to Big Garth and Odo, as they followed the path Lucky had taken up the rocky shore from the water. He felt like he wanted to punch them since they did nothing to keep him from being thrown into the sea.

"Welcome back, old friend." Odo reached out for him, but Brody just glared.

"Now you're calling me friend? Why didn't you remember that when Old Man Muck was making me walk the plank? Where is that traitor anyway? I want him to look into my eyes when I kill him."

"Brody, please, no," begged Gwen, reminding him of his promise to stop acting like a pirate.

"Muck is dead," Rowen told him.

"He is? Who killed him?" Brody looked over to Big Garth who had skill with the knife since he was the ship's cook. "Was it you, Big Garth?"

"It was Lucky," said Garth.

"Lucky?" Brody couldn't believe his ears. Lucky was Muck's best friend.

"I did it to keep him from killing Maggie," said Lucky in his gravelly voice. He rubbed the scar running across his throat.

"Maggie?" asked Gwen.

"My brother, Reed's wife," explained Rowen. "Lucky's turned a new leaf, and I've let him stay on as part of the crew. Brody, I sent them out looking for you, and told them not to come back until they found you. I left right after my brother's wedding, searching the coast for you as well. My journey led me here, and I'm glad it did. My new first mate is aboard the Sea Mirage, but it's yours again, now that I've found you."

"I – don't think so," he said, looking at Gwen as he spoke. "I've made a promise to Gwen to stop being a pirate."

"Then you're in luck," said Rowen. "The crew is all going to reform."

"What do you mean?" Brody looked over to the pirates.

"That's right," said Odo. "Rowen's going to set us up on a trade route."

"We'll be the crew of a trade ship from now on," said Lucky, getting to his feet.

"It'll give us all more time to find wives and start families of our own," added Big Garth. "I actually wouldn't mind the change."

"That's great," said Gwen. "Then you can join them, Brody."

"Gwen, I don't need a ship anymore. Your father gave me his ship."

"Where is it?" asked Big Garth.

"Is it as fast as the Sea Mirage?" asked Odo.

"It's right there." Brody pointed to the Desperado. The old, damaged ship creaked and groaned in the wind as it thunked against the pier.

"That's your new ship?" Big Garth burst out laughing.

"I think we'll be able to walk faster than that thing will sail," added Odo.

"It's been in a storm and hit by lightning," Brody explained. "But I'm going to fix it up, and it'll be as good as new soon."

Rowen's sea hawk swooped through the sky and landed atop the broken mast of the ship.

"We're going to use it to find my brothers," added Gwen.

"Where are they?" asked Odo. "In Hell?"

All three of the pirates laughed at that.

"I think it's a noble gesture," said Rowen. "Now that I'm living at Whitehaven Castle and have another ship, I won't need the Sea Mirage. You're welcome to use it to find Gwen's brothers, Brody."

"Thank you. I'll think about it," said Brody. "I have a lot of decisions to make soon."

"You're also welcome to stay at Whitehaven with me," said Rowen.

"Whitehaven?" Gwen looked up in surprise. "In a castle?"

"Aye," said Rowen. "Is there something wrong with that?"

Gwen and Brody exchanged glances. "I'm not sure we belong there," said Brody. "We're just . . . simple fisherman." He smiled at Gwen when he said it.

"Then stay with me," offered Edwin. "If you don't want to stay at the inn, you can use our house in town. Since my brother and his wife mainly stay at the inn now, too, the house is empty most of the time."

"Thank you. We'd like that," Brody answered.

"When's the wedding?" asked Rowen.

"I'm not sure," said Brody. "Hopefully, as soon as possible."

"I can contact the local priest from the church if you want," offered Edwin.

"Does he marry ex-pirates?" Brody felt as if he were an outcast in his hometown.

"There's no need to bother the priest," said Rowen. "I'm still a captain. If we hold the wedding on a ship on the water, I can do it for you right now."

"Gwen?" asked Brody, gazing into her bright, blue-green eyes.

"Let's do it," she said. "I only have one request, and I don't want any of you to laugh when you hear it."

Chapter 10

Brody held his head high as he recited his vows of marriage, standing aboard the Desperado. It had been a struggle to get the ship away from the pier. Honestly, he wasn't even sure it wouldn't sink before they finished.

They'd used the Sea Mirage to pull it out into the deeper water. Now, all the crew watched from the other ship in amusement. Only Edwin, Rowen, Big Garth, Odo, and Lucky were aboard the broken-down barge with Brody and Gwen.

"Well, you're married now, Brody. How does it feel?" asked Rowen.

"I'm not sure."

"That's because he didn't kiss the bride," called out one of the pirates from the Sea Mirage.

"That's right; you haven't kissed me yet as your wife." Gwen looked up with a wide smile. She was the most beautiful woman he'd ever seen.

"Then how about a kiss?" Brody kissed her deeply and then swept her off her feet, holding her in his arms as she threw back her head and laughed. Her long hair fluttered in the breeze.

"Look what I found," said Lucky, walking out of the cabin with a black hat in his hand that was worn by pirates.

"Where did you find that? It must have been my father's, but I've never seen it before," Gwen told them.

"It was right there in plain sight in the cabin," said Lucky.

"Really, Lucky?" asked Brody. "I find that hard to believe since Gwen's never seen it before." Brody put Gwen on her feet and sauntered over to Lucky.

"Sure, it was, Cap'n. Here, try it on for size." Lucky plopped the hat on Brody's head.

Brody straightened it and then kept walking forward, while Lucky kept backing up to the sidewall. Brody could see part of the sidewall wavering in the breeze, ready to fall apart. "Where did you find it, Lucky? If you're going to remain as part of the crew, you need to start telling the truth."

"And stop stealing," added Rowen.

Lucky's hand flew to the scar on his throat that Rowen had given him years ago when he caught him stealing. "All right, all right," he said, backing up and trying to get away from Brody. "I might have found it at the bottom of a trunk. Under the bed."

"That's what I thought." Brody stopped when Lucky's back was against the broken part of the ship's wall. "There's just one more thing I have to do before I forgive you for your part of my mutiny, Lucky."

"Anything. Anything at all, Cap'n," said Lucky.

"Go jump in the sea, just like I had to do."

"Me? Jump?" Lucky looked over his shoulder at the waters below him.

"Need a little help?" Brody stomped his foot, pretending to dart at Lucky. Lucky closed his eyes and turned his head, leaning back hard on the sidewall. Then the broken part gave way, and he fell into the sea.

Shouts of laughter and clapping went up from the crew on the Sea Mirage. Lucky surfaced, spitting a stream of water from his mouth.

"There. Now I feel better." Brody removed the hat and handed it to Gwen. "But I don't want to wear the hat of a pirate anymore. You take it."

"I'll take it, but not as a remembrance of my father," said Gwen. "I choose to remember him as a fisherman and will think of him that way until I go to my death."

"Then why are you keeping it?" asked Brody.

Gwen smiled. "I'll keep it as a remembrance of the day I met you. Also as a reminder that you promised to change."

"I don't understand," said Odo. "Your father's hat will remind you of Brody?"

"It's symbolic," she told them, stroking the hat with

her fingers. "It'll remind me of the day we fished a man out of the sea - a man who is now a fisherman and a tradesman. When I first saw Brody emerge from the fog it was magical and mystical. And the last thing I'd have ever expected was that someday I'd fall in love and be married to the *Pirate in the Mist*."

Epilogue

Five years later

Brody climbed the rigging of the Desperado with his four-year-old son, Breckon strapped to his chest. Gwen stood on the deck, shading her eyes, looking up at them with a scowl on her face. She cradled their newborn baby Katlyn in one arm, while with her other hand she held onto their son, Eric who one and a half years old. Their three-year-old daughter, Genevieve, was playing on the deck. Edwin and his wife, Marta, and their children were also aboard the docked ship.

"Be careful with Breckon," Gwen shouted up to Brody. "That is too high. He's going to fall."

"Bloody hell, Wife, he's strapped to my chest, and I've got my arms around him," Brody shouted back, knowing it was no use. He sighed and headed back down. Gwen was never going to let him teach their children the joys of sailing.

"She looks good," said Edwin. He leaned on the bulkhead, popping a nut into his mouth. "Of course, she should look good since it took you five years to fix up the old barge."

"What did you say?" Gwen glared at him.

Edwin held his hands in the air as he stood up straight. "The ship. I'm talking about the ship, not you," he told her.

Brody laughed. "I was a little preoccupied with raising a family, in case you haven't noticed." Brody jumped to the deck and unstrapped Breckon, letting the boy run around with the other children.

"Breckon, be careful," Gwen shouted out. "The deck might be slippery."

"I'll watch the children," said Marta, holding out her hand and taking Eric with her.

"Thank you," said Gwen, rocking the baby.

"I thought you two were going to try to find your brothers," Edwin said to Gwen. "Isn't that what you said when you first got married?"

"We did say that," answered Brody. "But then I was busy fixing the ship, and then the babies came along, and I guess it just didn't happen."

"I haven't forgotten about it," said Gwen. "I think of my brothers every day. Brody, I believe it's time we set out to find them."

"Nay," said Brody. I'll go, but not with you. It's not safe on the sea, and especially not with pirates. You need to stay here and watch our children."

Before Gwen had the chance to respond, Edwin stood up, looking at a ship that approached the dock. "I wonder who that is."

"That's the Sea Mirage," said Brody. "Rowen must be here for a visit. I wonder why." Brody hurried from the ship with the others following.

Gwen cradled her baby, and once again held little Eric's hand as Marta, and all the children followed her, making their way to greet their visitors. Once the Sea Mirage docked, Gwen saw Rowen exit the ship, helping an old woman down the ramp to the pier.

"Rowen, what brings you here?" asked Brody, rushing over to greet his good friend.

"Nairnie was the one who wanted to visit," said Rowen. "I think I'll let her explain why."

"Nairnie," repeated Gwen, walking over to greet them with her children in tow. "Why does that name sound familiar?"

The old woman looked up at her, and tears filled her eyes.

"Nairnie, this is my wife, Gwen, and these are our children," said Brody.

"Aye, I can see Cato in the bairns," said the old woman in her Scottish burr, hobbling toward her.

"You knew my father?" asked Gwen in surprise.

"I happened to mention your late father's name," said Rowen. "When I did, Nairnie about took off my head for not mentioning it five years ago."

"Nairnie," Gwen repeated the name, searching her memory until she remembered. "I know where I've heard that name before. My grandfather mentioned it once when I was a child. I thought it was the oddest name I'd ever heard."

"Yer grandfaither mentioned me?" The old woman stretched her neck and looked around. "Where is he?"

"Oh, my grandfather died when I was young," said Gwen.

"Guid thing, or I would have killed the bastard," said Nairnie under her breath.

"Pardon me?" asked Gwen.

"What about yer grandmathair?" asked Nairnie. "Did he ever mention her?"

"My grandmother died when I was a child too," said Gwen.

"Nay she didna die, child."

"She did. I remember it clearly," Gwen protested.

"What ye remember is the death of a woman ye were told was yer grandmathair. But yer grandmathair is still alive and kickin', lassie."

"I don't know what you mean." Gwen shifted the baby in her arms.

"I'm yer real grandmathair," said Nairnie. "Cato was my son, stolen by his father when Cato was just a child."

"You – you are?" For some reason, Gwen didn't doubt it for a minute. She felt it in her heart that it was true. "So . . . you're . . . family."

Nairnie nodded her head, tears rolling down her wrinkled cheeks. "Come here, Gwen." Nairnie spread out her arms. "I want to look at my granddaughter."

Gwen rushed to the old woman, and hugged her, crying because of the happiness in her heart.

"Ye have Cato's eyes," said the woman, reaching up to wipe away Gwen's tear. "Rowen told me he died. I only wish I could have been here to see my boy one last time before he left this world forever."

"His grave is just over that hill," said Brody. "Would you like to see it?"

"I would," she said with a nod.

The entourage headed up the hill to where Cato Fisher's body was buried, marked with a wooden cross made from the mast of his ship.

Nairnie fell to her knees atop the grave, throwing her body on the ground that covered her dead son. "Oh, Cato, I never stopped lovin' ye," she said, tears streaming down her face. "I wish I had come to look for ye," she said. "I'll never forgive myself for no' comin' after ye."

"Brody, take the baby," said Gwen, giving Katlyn to him, and getting to her knees as well. She lovingly wrapped her arms around her grandmother. "Please, don't cry, Grandmother."

"Nairnie, get off the ground," said Rowen, helping the old woman to her feet.

Nairnie took Gwen's face in her hands. "Aye, ye are a bonnie young lassie. I'm sure Cato was proud of ye."

"You're Scottish," said Gwen. "That means I'm Scottish too."

"Ye and all yer bairns. Brody, let me hold my great-grandchild."

Brody gave her the baby, and when he did, Nairnie's eyes lit up.

"You have four great-grandchildren," Gwen told her. "Children, come meet your great-grandmother." Gwen introduced Eric, Breckon, and Genevieve to Nairnie. The old woman looked so happy that is made Gwen's heart sing.

"Cato never had a son?" asked Nairnie, making sure to run her hand over the head of each child in a loving manner.

"Aye, he had three sons," said Brody.

"Three?" Nairnie looked around. "Where are my grandsons?"

"My brothers, Mardon, Tristan, and Aaron are not here," said Gwen.

"Well when will they be back?" asked Nairnie, poking her finger at the baby, trying to get Katlyn to smile.

"Nairnie, they left many years ago, and Gwen hasn't seen them since," said Brody.

"They're pirates," added Gwen.

"Pirates?" Nairnie's eyes flashed in anger. "No grandchildren of mine are goin' to be pirates."

"My father was a pirate, too," Gwen told her.

"Cato? A pirate?" Nairnie's mouth pursed, and her

eyes turned to slits. "I would have tanned his behind for that one. Nothin' guid ever comes from pirates."

Brody coughed purposely, and Rowen shook his head in a silent warning not to challenge Nairnie.

"Nairnie, did you forget that both Brody and I were pirates at one time?" Rowen gently reminded her. "We didn't turn out that bad, did we?"

"I suppose ye're right," she said, giving the baby back to Gwen. "All right, I'm ready. Let's go."

"Go?" asked Gwen "You just got here. Why do you want to go home when I've just met you?"

"Home? Who said anythin' about goin' home?" asked Nairnie. "I'm talkin' about goin' out to look for my grandsons, Mardon, Aaron and Tristan. And when I find them, I'm goin' to give them an earful. No grandchild of mine is goin' to be a pirate if I have anythin' to say about it."

"Nay, you're not coming on the trip," said Brody shaking his head. "A ship is no place for an old woman. Plus, pirates are dangerous."

"Say what ye want, but I'll no' lose three grandsons after I lost my only son. I willna repeat my mistakes, do ye hear me? We are goin' after them."

"We'll talk about this later," said Gwen, putting her arm around Nairnie. "Right now, we have a lot of catching-up to do. How long can you stay?"

"My work is done with the girls," said Nairnie. "So, I have all the time in the world."

"The girls?" asked Gwen.

"She's talking about my sisters, Spring, Summer, Autumn, and Winter," said Rowen. She's looked after them as a guardian to each of them until they were married."

"That's right," said Nairnie, nodding her head. "And now that I found my true family, I'm no' about to stop doin' what I do best."

"Nairnie, you're getting up in years," Rowen reminded her. "You've been through a lot, and it might be better if you leave the search to the men and stay here with Gwen and the children instead."

"Stay here? With me? Nay, I'm going as well," said Gwen. "Brody, don't even try to talk me out of it. Now Nairnie, let's go to the cottage and get a bite to eat. I'll tell you all about the children, and you can get to know them."

"All right, but they'd better no' try to leave without us," said Nairnie, flashing a warning glance to the men.

"We wouldn't dream of it," said Rowen with a chuckle.

Brody looked over to Rowen after the women walked away. "We wouldn't dream of it? You're not suggesting we take women along on our search for three nasty pirates are you?"

"Of course not," said Rowen, flashing a smile. "I was just giving you time to think of a way to tell them the news that we're leaving without them."

"Me?" asked Brody, not anxious to go up against two head-strong women. "I can't do it."

"Well, you'd better think of something to say to them. Now come on, I'm starved. I hope you have something to eat in that little cottage of yours."

Brody shook his head and followed Rowen, wondering how his young bride and the old woman were going to feel about this mission once they hit their first storm at sea.

Pirate in the Mist: Brody

Made in the USA
Middletown, DE
18 April 2018